# SUCKER JUNE

# Also by Sean Kilpatrick

*Gil the Nihilist: A Sitcom*

*Anatomy Courses* (with Blake Butler)

*fuckscapes*

# SUCKER JUNE
## Sean Kilpatrick

LAZY FASCIST PRESS

**LAZY FASCIST PRESS**
PO Box 10065
Portland, OR 97296

www.lazyfascistpress.com

Cover photo of Joy Pollak by Anna Serrone

Cover design by Matthew Revert
www.matthewrevert.com

Selections appearing, thanks to the editors: *Sleepingfish, New York Tyrant, The Quietus, No Colony, The Lifted Brow, Spork, Tarpaulin Sky, Sir!, Pindeldyboz, Lamination Colony, No Posit, 5_Trope, Libra/Libera, The Volta: Medium, 3AM Magazine, Cthulhu Sex,* and *NANO Fiction*

Printed in the USA.

# STRIP
# BISMARCK

The librarian refused to recognize any aspect of herself others did first. Her mother stuck some scars to a flagship middle-American birth even the eighties wouldn't spruce up. She hailed from a church she mispronounced and felt equivocal about stirrups. The baby peeled her off with a gesture unsure about its dustier territory. Tantamount with her gender, choice became muted to the unfortunately presentable world. But no one told her she was special until puberty brought the simulacrum of this effect through revolving male hormones. By then, all she could muster to rebel was the categorization of their shitty and shifting wants. She read too much into the sky. If she guessed herself habituated alongside the institution of another person, they'd be her coda. Earth wasn't big enough for the suicide she was planning.

She hopped a curb where the gentrification cooled down to a utopic blend and awaited the neighborhood children with which she had developed an implicit repartee of give me this and maybe next time. The streets were quiet, except for the occasional and perfunctory screaming. She liked to hear the city call her names. It was the only real parenting she got. She had to incessantly rotate the ability to empathize from her head in order to survive. There is no worse off because we're already in it. It's okay. The incalculable masks that go into a timesheet are okay.

The newspaper printed her singles ad for the ominous and geriatric. She enticed portly gentlemen to pay for dinner and stole their stories with an almost mimicked respect. Men demurred to her absconding with their greatest and most vain efforts. The omission of her lips from an intimate scenario revoked it in her favor, delegating whoever she was with to tussle for their own arousal without the inclusionary benefit of foreplay. Even a husband found himself counseled tacit to her neck. He was progressively staved off once she realized he was the result of her believing her own pillow talk. The kind of man who changed anything to get married. She required more agency than there was space for in a bedroom. Someone with the perfect balance of indifference and obsession half concerning her. She only said I love you if you obligated her to for months and had finally given up. The individual rejections she would wand about never parsed how little she had been raised. I never been hungry on food. I just eat to resent being fed.

She didn't know whose loss brought people toward her, theirs or hers, or their sense of hers, or their indignation at her preferring her own loss to anyone else's. She only hoped that she wasn't so alone in her incontinence. Her husband paid a psychotic amount of attention to detail. She evaded being monitored even during sleep. She startled conscious between snores if someone was admiring her. Her father had scared her of the need to be watched over. He was a loafing doofus mad from lack of her. She would often wake next to a man who was crying to be held. Her husband stayed home with his idea of their kid. He had degrees in different fields and applied constantly to every job, even fast food, and was rejected because of how intensely she wanted him to work. It wasn't about money or status, it was about him going away from her, about opening a space where she could begin with someone new. He took up fast food anyway. He ate so much of it their bed was mostly oil. All in her hair, fingerprints of the tribe grabbing it.

She purchased everything. Her husband was just a figment of the house she bought. His apnea was his biggest contribution. His undying affection made him worse than any neighbor. He would go at their lawnmower until she was sick of explaining him to her family. He failed to engage any gathering. He just wanted to punish her for her not being a kid in the woods with him. No amount of returned affection appeased his severely impractical notion of the word love. She regretted ever having said it back. Saying it meant nothing anyway. The concept was as fake, if not an onus of, the subsequent ritual of marriage. You couldn't blurb the derivationally abstract to feel better about how it always fizzled regardless. Why did she route herself to these locales for the propaganda of fine living? Out of spite, of course, for the conditions that made any form of escape both so necessary and ultimately so unobtainable. People had for many years been reduced to decoration.

She established dating website profiles and wrote easygoing, as if this was an accomplishable trait. DTF, easygoing, serious Christian, but she was none of those things. What she was when she went on a date was approachable, but highly armed. What had been done to her was a status she would refract through everyone's plaintive conceit that caring was indeed possible. She told herself she didn't need anyone until the boy or girl hurt as a consequence of her faulty conviction was forced to scare up some recompense. Anyone who doesn't need love should need the police if they mean to frivolously test their theory out. She needed those foolish enough to love her distributed to different area codes and bussed in when she could stomach the idea of them. She made you accept any yielded act with a bigger gratitude than her issues with it beforehand might elaborate. She had reduced her husband's entire input to brief conventional patter. They only stumbled over an occasional glimpse of what they could have been, self-sabotaged because she hated this other person she was fashioning him into. What a sick method of eschewing responsibility, his being so emotionally supportive every attack belonged to her.

Her husband cashed out his student loans to help her do nothing she couldn't have done on her own. It was mostly spent on fun meals to apologize to her for being himself. Everyone that looked at her wanted to give her a job. She needed folks to think they needed her. Secretly, she couldn't care less how they may have murdered themselves doing so. But she worked extra hard because it was important to display yourself as a contributor. Her husband had no vigilance for how he was perceived. He cut his hair with a kitchen knife. He was such an expert at being supportive he had no place in society. She couldn't imagine his potential in any corporeal sense and had forgotten what made him seem spiritually relevant. Maybe it was because he went to the bathroom too many times a day. She had taken to his vastly welcoming parents with a perverse etiquette. She fantasized about them letting her be their caretaker. She was only seen through slips of light even by those who studied hardest. She never condemned a singular location to thoughts amassed to inflict more her. The air would hang. She saw information on any topic as her enemy, wanted things relayed as a sphinxlike riddle or got bored. She had never performed research once, but was afloat with so much conjecture from the coterie she inspired that everything was known and known brighter.

She learned to speak from the tooth auto-erotically extracting itself from her skull. That's how your god would gum you, with hemophilic blasphemes to its image. Once between forever she and her husband crapped out on the expectations of their union in order to enjoy each other's presence. She wasn't busy making this impossible with other men. He wasn't busy picturing who those men could be, if they weren't already near. They shared a frolic without code. They were aware of the illness of events outside and were thus prepared for pregnancy against those odds. They'd feed their baby its own glossolalia. It would muscle through a conga line of other it to rebuild the lies they knew. They would send it into the canned matter of other viable heads and claim whatever backwash. It felt uselessly evil enough to repair their feelings. The barbeques they wished they jumped into. They were doing it to appreciate silence again.

Another them they pretended wouldn't die in the same position. We have to put up curtains on our adventure or they'll ban our DNA.

Her alias barely encored. It rang like unintentionally divulged information, clandestine and presidential, as if someone had earned their hernia a reputation. I'm going to give you some worse moles if you step near me, the librarian was evermore forced to whisper. She bided herself thin to better hurt women's feelings. They either kept stock or tended to the legitimate syndrome of their keys. I don't enjoy standing up for myself. I just want to inflict pain at the grainiest portent of legal provocation. You gotta have the perspective to explode. I'm like one of these connoisseurs that take their hemorrhoid to show and tell. Get a bigger car because of it. She admired the authenticity of her badass friends retreating to motherhood from the Charley horse of a hotly partied-out life. It made her want to etch out her clit. People would leave you alone, but first you had to provide them a semblance, even if it was just another cloned you.

Her husband dwelled like a teenaged ghost with parents too overly kind to prolong the suicide he tried for for ten years, and she couldn't take the expectation that he might continue putting it off a moment longer because of feelings she had let him accrue. She dreamt a series of accountants were nudging her. The dread someone else's pleasure can crank into your sleep. You wake up trying to determine where you should be and afraid of ever arriving there. She requested that he wait himself out pensively until a session was okayed, then ignored him, sleeping nude. As long as the men who doted on her couldn't get off. As long as she had a nonpartisan trove. Sex made her feel like a victim, and she shut down during, in subtly alarming ways. Her eyes filmed over. She had a robot pose mid-coitus that the exceedingly sensitive geeks she courted would try to talk her out of. Men she left ran a lighter over her stockings to return the smell. She was beautiful to the extent that they did what she asked without her having to manipulate her face into a practiced kindness. They escorted her their confidence until she didn't need her own. She had scars. She didn't need confidence.

She lied the amount a wife had to, surrounding her husband with transients she had had affairs or tension with to see how someone inherently antisocial could further wilt. She did that so many times he only spoke once a day. He fawned over her whenever the anger at being relatively dismissed subsided. He wanted her to feel worshipped, to guide them higher in compliance with the pedestal. She was not interested in his take on her, or her greatness, or their contaminate potential. She wanted to be hosted by various lesser partially-interested parties. It was revenge because she felt upstaged by his hatreds.

They took their simple predilections for each other's racket outside and stepped all over everything possibly sacred about that, with creels of insect gossip. They inflicted generosities block by block to uphold the ice-thin pretense no one would get pillaged. They couldn't somehow build themselves into this immaculate representation of a type of human that had and will never exist. The citizen you scratched out your eyes to be.

Whites liked blanketing separate from their ability to brag about danger. Their money reeked of the instantly obsolete items that crowbarred them from it. They liked being disassembled enough to nearly live. There was a modicum of relevance they could overdo now that their handheld electronics were without batteries. Another man's wife might tap her shoulder as if to request directions from the adultery.

The only bystanders he had reluctantly spent time with were raucous in a store-bought way. They ruled over his abnormality throughout high school with a combined sense of their boisterous selves and a disguised adherence to the common. In time, he was left behind, baffled by their typical adult lives because they had been the poor sole examples of anyone halfway smart or charming around him. The women were loud, openly mocked him, repeated his name like a basic treachery, cheated on their pretentiously devoted boyfriends, took that contagion to his first girl, who translated different boys with her free-spirit. Their shitty attitudes, condescending assistance, and unexplainable backstabbery had covertly fucked his life. What angered him most was, even in domesticity, they still upheld the fantasy of their own uniqueness. They imagined themselves capable of art within such colonized lives. He didn't consider anyone a sellout. He was aware there was no dodging money. He just didn't think they should be so insultingly proud of who they were and so readily ashamed for him. He had never experienced pride. How could he, knowing mostly them? But what community would have cured how he felt since birth? It goes wrong no matter who. Beleaguered in that former circle when he found his wife, she was the first brilliant person he'd met. Talented, witty, of a higher class, sharp and spot-on mean only when called for, not to assert herself needlessly or to dominate a room, quiet, someone like him, less redundantly in charge, not perpetually screaming her first thought as a gift to her constituents like every female he'd met before, not the same nasty, amateur Hannibal Lecter everyone with an ounce of intelligence practiced being in a faux cosmopolitan tenor, but a real and humble getter of it, and this angel, finally, because of him, of course, in the long run, was indifferent. His wife had been around so many types she informed him his childhood friends were of an unsubstantiated variance, but he had given up thinking anyone was worth attention, besides her. He was addicted to the sugar in her waste. She was driven by that to seek others. It was in her magnificent character to explore variables and he resented her for it. She couldn't remain good to him from such a height. He would fill the gap between them with violence. First against himself, against the idea of her in himself, now in wonder against the populace. The crimes they'd do were lettered in the sky.

He was doing a voice. He did voices when she allowed him some complacency. The last thing a girl wants to be in a relationship is liked. Then she'd have to chafe wearing you. But I'm upright silken, he said. I'm shy as skim milk. She went to the bathroom for him. He rested in wonder between her knees, slowed her hand over the dabbing paper. She dotted and he used it to chloroform himself. I wanna fuck your first and middle names exchanged. I've read enough books to lose all my meaning. She rubbed her saliva in. He was eternally examining her with the reverence of a fifteen year old. She nodded on him till he got acrid. He towed benign spasms from her spot. They drifted against the fridge, bracketed with takeout. Her bust had chicken skin, nipples defined by manufactured freeze. Every time he came another twin got roosted in her. She liked allowing this to work and wondered how long she might continue allowing anything. If their children pointed at her coming out, she would stay.

He pictured harming vertebrates so regularly he was already an expert. She reserved hate for herself and those who bothered gestating her. His apologies were the prime occurrence between them. He brought a skinned rabbit up by its ears and into boiling water. He had no clue if this method was pertinent or sanitary. The concept felt robust. He preferred what they ate to have the eyes still in. The skin became so clouded and mushy it was like swallowing how good she looked without enterprise. She saw how important it was for him to feed her, that he had lost his way being no longer able to hand her a menu. She selected gracefully as her curvature. It used to be how she paid him back. Such the chancre of the wed, to find their waiter.

Tissues matted sublunar along the rim of her belly button, the finery he retired in, the filaments he'd tamp rhyming. When she was holding out, he resented her scars because he wanted to be responsible for them. The marks on her body were so attractive you missed the pleasure of seeing them made. She was still in the manner of skittering on him, letting him be an owl on her sphincter when the orgasm waved. They were a kind of halo underneath the snake, of it and brought whereby, partaking, but able to isolate each other. They liked being watched while producing partly chilled fluids. Not to be outdone, and equally afflicted, her husband took to murder, not by technical skill, but by his veracity and aesthetic valuing of the act. They migrated on foot, through the ghettos that toyed them in with just enough things to like, enough downhome community to keep the violence occasional, but underwhelming.

Her husband spoke obsessively of his body and the many superficial perturbations he was shocked to have at merely thirty. The uninterrupted and untreatable piles, the tenacious ringworm scored about a steadily dribbling penis doctors had promised was uninfected, slapping down useless and expensive creams and antibiotics that exacerbated the issue, the patchy skin rubbing off wherever water landed, the uncanny pain pinballing between kidneys and prostate, the sprained muscles from yawning, the staggering dendrites, the teeth that would splinter if he chewed anything, mouth ordinarily full of blood, the technologically profound and roving tinnitus, the teetering between constipation and diarrhea in defiance of diet, two full rolls of toilet paper to efficiently clean the area, the frayed nerves causing random physical panic attacks, nothing to do with any current incident, as if real worse malfunctions were demandingly afoot, so he had to stop thinking to breathe, had to audition his breath. One day an ear stopped working. He commanded his body to transact or upend. When he blew his nose, his balls inflated. It was a daily impersonation of how she felt about him, this limbic crack war, and he blamed her because whenever she recapitulated he either blocked his maladies out or they went away for certain. If he took up a habit, or found entertainment, the machinery involved would break. His car surrendered any possible savings. He was irrevocably trapped behind these problems and they would only take on age. He needed someone to screw this information into and asked for medical advice from the freshly captured. If there was a hint of dismissal, he got their nose. He warped cartilage with his palm until it ballooned outward from an occlusion on the head. When this exercise had been accomplished plenty, he never showed symptoms again.

She was absolved of shelter, thus hydra-headed Voltron manipulations to accumulate a passable male from the many cooping her less proportionate than their individual grotesqueries weren't necessarily exploited by the batch in order to create a self-custodial rift from that gender's girdling need. Everything she did with just one man was to oblige him, because he alone could never be expelled from her disappointment at any consecrated labor, this vanity for the perfection of her libido, his single incidental talent she invariably consoled against her will. Everyone outright healthy seemed to demand a home from their more acclimated boy. A bed had never been an issue for her and was certainly not reliant upon any partner. Still, she bricked her guys into a diminishingly tangible support system. A platter of them would suffice in transition. She bestowed injunctions on each pause to insist the act was futile, because it conclusively had been, up to now, unimproved by any level of orgasm. The orgasm itself was an exclusionary adventure. She came delinquent of her lover's versatility and often in spite of it. It was a trial, obscuring the practicality of what whoever assumed would work so she could focus on a corner of her mind to hush the invasion of someone other. She had only ever been taught to feel probed. No pennyante psychological harvesting would reverse this, especially if she profited from sham gallantries dressing up like love. How vital it was to prolong her Rubik's Cube sexuality became counterbalanced by the unprovoked denial of the kinder traits she truly, disastrously possessed. When her husband troubleshot her mood to rut his way deeper into an unachievable closeness, the room went transitory with policed neuroses. They should appoint each other the world's exception, he insisted. Whoever might sate her simultaneous whims was the phantom he coerced himself to be beneath the sheets. The dilemma was usually anyone's Herculean efforts classified how pedestrian they really were, or she'd call them that anyway, even if they secretly found success. Success was not forthcoming, particularly if it was, because male sexual success meant female vulnerability. But as soon as the roofs were gone she let herself be made to idiotically come and the others were too afraid to point. Now she'd squirt the positive elements of every tryst down through one and it didn't matter how boringly alpha he was or how defectively sensitive, or the money in between those categories, or the paranoia of objects once perceived.

She let her chaperon supervene if the episode mocked itself appropriately. Funny to watch her body laid on from wherever she went during. The fungal sweat of various men had fouled the skin of her torso, as if their shadows had skimped over partway, too lazy to climb back off. She was cruel to her person after that. Unknown soups ensued. She self-injured in an act of rage meant to seem promised for the falsely accused, effectively silencing her husband's suspicions. When she granted him rare access, he gorged an immediate come due to deprivation while she conjured blueprints for the crane that would lift him from her. She occasionally participated by using him to masturbate, mumbled shut up and moved him in accordance with her hand. She did this to everyone, actually, probably because of some minor but untreated venereal bacteria which had grown to keep her semi-impotent. He carried her to preserve her childlike feet.

She was sick of having her gravity explained. She geared the line toward the peninsula without thinking. Everyone would follow her anyway, that's why she despised a map. They didn't need maps. Anything on you can spread. She incorporated people's rashes. They'd paint her alive for a day and happily disappear. She made a sound when she came like she didn't want it to happen, but that it was ultimately happening, despite everyone's efforts.

Her husband had taken her away from the streets with so much dour support she missed the streets. I used to be too kind to be hired. He had been screwing her dresser piecemeal in a way she could feel against her body in the fabrics. He unrolled the drapes in her, could climb into her mouth with that much light. The pussy pulse stars timelessness. A Pentecostal soy you shut your peepers in. I feel such the Picasso, she cooed at a procession of heads. Balder still and yours.

You look downright hirable in that suit. He meant she was naked and had absorbed in his beard. They resumed the necrophilia. A greyhound hurdled her hip and ottoman. She thumped the penciled muzzle, the ribs and pink crab meat she allegedly envied, and flicked whiskey into its beautifully innocent eyes. I work all day, she told it. I come home and am asked questions. Such lovingly patient questions and offerings of food and space I could take up rape. She felt like bleeding out on purpose. Everyone who mounts me outweighs me. How you fuck the smile off a cinder block? My generation never grew up tied to any railroad tracks, that's why we're too busy liking ourselves. Fear is all you have if no one fucked you up enough. Am I guy-level right yet? The greyhound was back at her. She grabbed the beak. Will you fucking marry me already? She pushed her wedding ring down its throat. It backed up, trying to suspend the object from its breathing, and vomited against the jukebox until her song came on.

Someone called me princess on this street. He was suffering an umbilical amount of heat at the time. Had she left the coffee pot in the library? He promised so much suicide would happen after I moved on. No one is punctual enough with making good on that topic. I bed a man like I'm in a rush to make whoever will follow him jealous. Wait, I'm still at work, miscarrying into the garbage disposal. I mean being alive for a second, a gnat in that whirring. The plumbing has rinds statelier than my life. Is my pop stardom secured because I forgot my clothes? She'd crack her elbow reversed like the movies everyone she dated liked. She obtained a fugitive gloss lasting long as a bubble and then her intestines were across the street and the poorly dubbed sound finally caught up.

She collaborated with her pills. Everything looked like a suppository anyway. Objects that went in her readjusted her breathing. Her muscles involuntarily rejected any penetration. So many men had mistaken this as an unprecedented tightness. It was just her panic and fleeting self-esteem. Her trauma had kegels. Being the sole catatonic cheerleader of what she felt she had to do, she took one for the team, consistently. It was her duty to be climbed on. No man or woman had coaxed the necessary featherweight appropriation of her freedom for the context of an orgasm. She did the splits on her medicine. Furtive upper abdominal bunching continuously exonerated her. Any item not nailed to the floor was something she could use to break herself with, and that love described her. Not since she proved she could leave her father's compound, eking the menial wages people without connections force their pride to endure, had she so admired the previous vanity of the job her lungs did. Before her man came along to void both their bowels.

She hung up her coat and checked voicemail. A little boy ran over and stapled his foreskin to the desk, presenting it to her, both arms up, victorious. That's why she masturbated with a ray gun that didn't permit climax. She quarterbacked herself with what she was denied, even if she was the one pulling the trigger. Cataloging maggot therapies, a stenciled debridement of the carpets below her, the library another job where they never chastised you for sitting down, she could feel the boy's skin crunching through the wood of the desk.

The first seizure put her nodding. Wrestling her panties in place, she felt that this, finally, was the entire prolonged function of her gender, but couldn't laugh. They danced on her position, solid for hours, struggling to see the wet or shedding state. She willed shit for self-defense. Nothing quacked loose. She hummed pee forth, banded around her thigh. They reinvigorated, outweighed her excessive workout pattern, stumping her core, stripping her buck. She was spanked to ramp her body kind: pudgy mechanism men steal. Cunt repairing with mucus, bruises an attributing pose the world would barter, the slab she felt below her tummy, the balling together of each germ that slid expelled in contrition with the mouth that gave it. She walked naked to her desk like the striding consulate of every published farce, retrieved a pair of binoculars, and held them in strewn close-up, the pores of those who tried ruining her. She paddled toward this day dissociated from any travel to it, petty actions there an excerpt of her amelioration.

The teensy carrots in her veins were fulminating with such cauterized information anyone with a dick had to hide. She wreathed cotton down her throat to emphasize who had been wearing it, fucked before creation like an appropriate slur. The atrocities vouched against her, born from the lack of others, were such impolite snot she could then triple in an evening. Nothing is brave if you have backup.

He remembered commenting drolly to his wife on some distant riot she instigated haphazardly. See, my genomes pet the solar system. I spent today cuddling our ultrasound. Appended my hand to a sidewalk raised by trees and stroked the rawer thoroughfare. I play at the park. Am guilty of its slides. I had fat sons before. Mapquest that shit. Who ain't raped titanic in they hand-me-downs?

He had come into muscles from dumpiness. The excess weight slowed him civil. Then a miraculous reckoning tallied his aerobics. She strained the blood from her ponytail, chopping it shorter. They followed constellations she was in the process of renaming. He'd invest in her slight furs, but the visual was too tempting. Whatever toxicology spurred them liked the cold. They read driver manuals aloud at night. It was like poetry now that cars were forgotten. She thought, glaring up, that they were enduring within some infinitely infected bowel that should never digest them.

He liked needling her shit out his cuticles, stroking the vaginal dent their fucking hoisted through the wall of her anus, doubly rhythmic froth they spelled their come to. She discussed god with him for the first time. Another twin was swatting toward awareness. This parasite gumming to portray the both of them with every sad expression. He placed her STDs under a black light. They weren't sure they had any. That's just how she viewed the relationship. He rimmed her like someone genuinely starved. She settled in his populace to kin their upstart. His first friends. She knew he caught in her immediately. There had been some years between the act and joy. She burbled as their foundling to encourage a third go. They ruffled an imitation of the puny, ignored diseases that were there before. Artillery is such a beautiful name for a baby. I hope it's born with no tongue. Oh, I hope a tongue transpires so it may scream, interminably, like its horrendously nubile parents.

There was cocaine left over in her spittle, a sole hereditary gift. The man she was abandoned with resented the dreams her presence made impossible to pretend might happen. He immersed them in the anti-government rhetoric of survival. The last shred of his envisioned importance went to process his erection, the lump that kept him crabby until he set her there. His worshippy presents scarcely phased her. Being taken through childhood stunted her sadness. Even her nausea at the act was under someone else's control. She cut her body and the planets aligned.

Offended by anything unleveled, she listened to the earth. It had always been saying revenge. Anyone's reason to hear otherwise was worthlessly personal. She believed her destruction to be a universal beneficiary. Her father's soiled voice vibrated underground. They had marred those traits bloodlines ago. He was in a wheelchair and clambered from it to nub her for several hours on a remote-controlled bed. She could see his heart hacking beneath yellowed skin, feel the veins clamoring to half-mast the cock he eventually rubbed a single hanging strand from, cold against her thigh. The hindrance of this much ejaculate broke the dentures out of his mouth. His white hair formed a synthetic impression of itself in her taste buds. He self-consciously rambled to her between sucking, alternating a critique of his appearance with past victories. She was in a trance, occasionally rocking back, pretending enjoyment. This was far from the rare events of her sometimes coming out of spite. She went somewhere no one could possibly one-hundred percent return from, if they returned at all. His skeleton dragged on her for a span outside what the rabble think is time progressing. It was not a bad feeling or any feeling. If you cried once, that would be your vocation.

The elements pardoned her translucent from the godliness she had been accused of. She was far too alien a creature to compete with this pejorative sky. She shook off weathers, clapped in the physicality of recollection. The absence prior to her belly, a chronic prod thanks to dad and his makeshift C-section, which was novice at best and had purportedly maimed her into infertility, more a mistrust of hospitals than a fear of being jailed for incest, returned despite the cold to prolapse her breathing. He kept her conscious through what he labeled an unveiling. She watched him dig the fissure full of property. The seismic pressure pubic hair to belly button took on a vigor almost pulmonary once the scalpel sought some thin-dicked payback. Blood didn't pool over until she coughed. She spent the next month repairing her own fever, praying by then for even more deformations than her son and brother had anyway survived. It was a runt she couldn't influence with language. She shunned it and took to cities, where noitas would get lost. Today the fetuses were juggling icicles inside her. She sensed her air fogging downward to them through the popsicle broth they outlived. They were climbing the back of her throat to utter themselves existent. She felt them gnawing from within her scars.

Her husband had anxieties about impressing her stable. Incensed with formalities, he took a second meal of his mouth. They ignored him, burping in picnic table rows by the gymnasium's poorly gathered heat. She sat between her father and their son, who was propped crooked in his wheelchair, issuing honks of approval at her hug. Her father regarded husbandry a measly stature. She was comparing him with a bumbling character in the only children's book he read to her. He told horror stories of the wayward teen who stooled her ready. The reunion with his daughter invalidated whoever she dragged along behind it.

Everything concerning her father that went so numb returned far more disfigured than she could refuse. She helped off her clothes until she recalled the indignation that this was their essential interaction. Her father noodled himself attending. She needed the image more than the obstacle of performing to have it made. No more playing dead, no trumped up suicides wielding his stockade love in tune with her sense of guilt. Any man's love will insulate you from victory. She had taken up library science to conserve as little of herself as possible. She punished who she was with information. Anyone with any intuition gets demoted by the facts. She was only peaceful if her background could have many alterations. She had given up on peace.

She introduced a fork vertical into her father's eyeball, prongs acting as a fulcrum to uproot the quaggy and bulking encasement by suction exterior the skull. The following ooze bisected threefold around his wince. It was the donation of an aperture to her nativity. His kind were always right next door. She squatted over him, taking his neck back at an incline, kissing wholly, and shat her lower intestines on the blade from the colon to her twins, across the pulley system he had left for lungs. Her husband entered, cheering new twins from the remaining objects that were her kin and they snagged their overgrown nails tight into the old man's flesh, leaning back until it snapped off in sunny mattings. He waggled a bare muscular system like someone being told, intake gargling decades of these now cleansed tries at food, the librarian's dysenteric lifespan snorkeling immortal through his each bronchi.

I want to be known for my rictus, he was fond of saying.

# WAXING KINGDOM THROUGH BENT POSTURES

The leaves she crawls through amuse her, always forward of her, the boot she posits from them mine. Piggyback the tree her unformed spine, slid not so gentle, piss a symbol that christens us. She plays with the bugs in her swaddling. The outline, extemporaneous of her cartridge, torso barely a splint, will yawn itself present around me. I took this bitch from my ribs like a scary malt. I'm lonely for how age will dilate her.

I masturbate in front of her. She peers right through the welfare of that commotion. I'm building the portrait a few years ahead every time she waves unfamiliar at my swinging cum. All my resources are in fluid. Splotches stung her a few months in. I chewed squirrel, fed her cute mulch between fevers. She would learn how unimportant it is to survive. I abandoned her in a pen, hiking counties over to kick a wet nurse into action, though she resented formula. Our ilk tends the natural over coals. I parlayed a habitual madness that would lend us certainty. I line her crib with porn. My luck I'll raise someone who can ultimately resist. She won't stay plenary with whoever considers health.

I provide an onset ass. This is the frottage we won't quite call TV. I shoot like the stars matter. My shaft would be normal outside her warmth, upon which the base expands triple, the head hulks some unattainable blood, foreskin disavowed to act a further layer of how thick. She will grow to venerate my quality circulation like a rattle answering back. I embark my girth, the monstrosity secluded all hers, delicacies timed by the throat, princess hymen till the minute I tour that trust. I'll suit her till she can't blink.

I coagulate too far in the presence of those wanted. I need her so unfortunately educated she understands tragedy en masse. She has to accept us as the loss of everything. I can only come inside someone better than I am, but they have to be made mine, to remember they're paramount cuz I say. All I want to jaw is the lint out my little girl, a chorus of her behind. I seem so common at the zipper. She scoots her project around an America deeper set to nut. I have to bang my erection in the cooler before it's a permanent jungle gym she'll candy with her first word.

We're in the woods where unattended crying doesn't stain the canopy. I could relocate her instincts same as any princess budding lithe. Her eyes are already the right amount dead. Are those the shadows you're named after, frisking themselves at the periphery? I'll give them your crib's password if you take to venture. I disembowel a rabbit at the speed she pops her bottle in and out, innards reverse-swallowed as the second performance of its drool. The contents outsizing her puppet how she'll dream. I loosen the thing plummeted through itself by some contrivance of life flexing in her pupil. As long as I don't scare her fear altogether dissolved.

Beyond yuppified suburbs, the newfangled gentrification they cloak, ghettos becoming more photogenic than threatening, we squat rural in a croaked trailer. I kill our groceries. She chips the scum off my fingers. We hitchhike to town. It's a birthday I'm allowing. An object a year from the factory crowd even my nightmares couldn't breach. I'll imprint some gender or hurting her won't be worth it. The copious sediment of what passes for sane in humans veering speech, I shield her ears. She'll be cute, my cutie, girlish without the commiserate squawk of vanity a community rigs in tow. She won't vamoose up the arrogance of her cunt's costuming as so many with their men leashed, wallet in teeth, sense of handheld confidence jokey for a semi-erection. Never worse than those who read a book and think they're free. They rebel their assembly to partake in its height. Whoever's lost for a profit, designer indignation for the caste they secretly pet, manhood reduced to the gym, faux-existential suit-wearers, layers of interfering parent curb the cum, skippy for a side, their infrequent conniptions naughtier than a franchise. I can't even smell a bitch with her own money. No one bosses you apt inside the official.

Rib by rib, there's increased space, bellybutton to sternum elongating new, the upcoming miracle loitering forth. I change her pink outfits until I have to taste what's under, hand along the fat outline in my pants everyone should hook their phone to, billow of her flesh telling me gather patience. Someone passing for a man, proud knickknack awaiting his supervisor's cluck, shaped like the glow of the screens that have castrated him, catches this through the partition and returns a look. I detain him in the enclosure.

Hey, you a hands-on type locust? Sop the aerosol of your fast food infected jissom in my daughter, genuinely. Stop stressing and get private with us. You the thug grown buttery up my cousin? – Here I'm blithely whacking the side of his skull into the rack for personal items. Ramp free both manageable inches and synchronize my sister. Watch how she straddles the counter as if to question your game. She's saying you're her fucking civilian. Don't trifle, motherfucker, be swift. It's free. My niece's crack ain't ready, but skin is skin, dude. Wait till I grow a collar, rotor-butch security knight. En garde twat to rear! Hawk a loogie on her like a capable statesman. What? You my busybody Greek? Psst, she's baby talking you, eat the retard out that pussy. Put those ebonics on your Doppler. I insist.

He's moved from a stutter to a sob. I glut my fist into his slowly malfunctioning carriage. He issues the curse of his family and begins vomiting. We a big 9-1-1 fan? I give him so much of my knuckles the cartilage in his nose joins with them. I spit another drapery over the pulp no longer in use. People never take their coffins rare. For the walk home, we sweat off his expensive blood. Next year, honey.

The creek guides our chores. We sucker the whole day to it. I sponge her near and dear. She's bathed in one pollution to the next. The water helps me raise her. That's why I resent nature. Everywhere you've been is the inch-wide blockade sequentially fencing you. I don't believe the air. Particles haven't occurred. I only worship how a gun works. Maybe energy's hooding ghosts who can't conform. The earth postures atmosphere so you never taste the sun discharging. Why else would I shut my eyes so hard to come?

I sneak up behind passersby. The farm a mile off seats a diminished, illiterate family. They'll die between the legs if any calls are placed. I trench in the warzone of every sex. I've become part of her scent to where she could be tracked between oceans. The attractive need to enjoy not being able to escape.

I cure her tears with a proper squint. I am ordained in her loving me back to the extent that my authority is unquestioned. She'll be catered for about her bleeding. I am starving open the periods. I'm really into how a progeny scatters the lining foremost incurred. I used to get cast in my vulnerabilities when love would slight me, a peon captive to his platter. Tricking myself as a lady's butler cramped us up. I wasn't sure someone returned the sentiment unless they perjured themselves against me. We were dogmatized of the same unchecked ostentation at my expense, conked through blackout honeymoons. No one wanted to bypass the terror with me, so I boomeranged in. The wares I brought back from the haze still excite me into the occasional bowel movement. It was like being handed the drugs that would later inform your autograph.

Long ago, I was ignorant enough to separate the word abuse from the process of living. You participate in your oppression by remaining alive. Life is an ununiformed war without pause. Birth clued me in, but I fancied a second of reprieve was possible with a girl. Then the fact love doesn't exist, that it's not near the lie our chemicals may practice soothing. The suddenness of died out love, the ease by which another's taken, entirely invalidates the initial procedure.

I marker lessons on the trailer's hull, nourish her tantrums, kind as the armed. Her lifespan's on a rack stretching lengthwise to my gullet. She will mature according to the openings I encourage. I will perfect the seed that has mistaken us. I will trample her with the necessary female stelliums so she can at least picture freedom. When she tries to opt out, I'm there with stitches. If I poach that mind well, she adores me the same as her scars.

She plods free because anything that might challenge us is immediately at the end of a scope. Another child has fortuned on her, rolling tandem through make-believe. He shovels her at his shorts. This is a portent of how any devotion will hang you. She's commenced the decoy of her own warmth. Thought I had my setup commandeered. Apparently I go too remote between the ears. I observe the frolic, her obscene gratification in his presence. I consider taking them both duped from their genes. An acquiescence to this impulse will carry her from me anyhow. No friendly wizard could saw away all that whore.

I totter from the woods, beard pinned under a hound mask, howling bubba coos. I tickle them with woofs and bitch tricks like they paged a fool who really cared, rest him on my knee for lovey dovey antics, the weakness heartfelt babble does display. I tilt the boy's rascally face against the slits pressed for air, resuscitating the shortness of his gasp, and clamp the rubber down onto his lips, grinding out a mass between the plastic and his scream. Our materials hailing a liquidity choked freeform, banding a formal digestion in parentese, his head the tapestry snapped apart to my gut, first-class yum epitomizing colossal when I feed. His kicking me is as involuntary as the rest of him. I squeeze the throat until everything attached below ejaculates onto my pretend snout. He wobbles free of the things he's ever eaten. I brandish him sallow by the legs, gulping a coin-sized, intermittently soiling penis between the costume's rip where my fangs now glimmer. Covered in him, we're covered; she will believe. I am a parasite and I miss my host.

She's Zeze, boobs fracturing in, cresting lidless, spigots penumbra, sanctum where slaver curves dialed, ass communally unavoidable, foot she drums outside ligament, doing the splits twenty-four seven. I tell her bunny. She springs about the house. The purest downy whiff of prepubescence goddamn subdued. She gets in the camera's face, unacknowledged breadwinner of her handstands. I okay the tapes. I'm willing to hustle any idea as long as no one touches it. Her epileptic inventions array, dimensional fetching in the liner. She's so profound I forget who spawned who. She throttles her bare self. The hymen's in place, fused seamless. Her her-colored asshole yet blackened. I've been beyond monk. I fuck like I'm trying to X-out the world me first. But I'll wallop no one until it's her. Not a pledge, it's all my lungs.

Barak'll tutor a cunt for chump change. He goes canker on the pastoral. Slaves by the decimal. There's no art to the graveyards he'll expand. His prodigy ruins the objective: she's poured, unmannered, out of herself. She chimes in, debuts an assessment, despite that no hospital awaits her haywire remarks. The man bothers his dogs, a slave a month, tasteless cruelty, before she has the chance to learn. What's the reward without their believing consent? Zeze never scrubbed matronly advice from these. Barak sears his property where the thighs meet.

If someone explained her victimhood, Zeze would laugh them out of court. She is riddled with my intent, voluntarily harmonized. We discuss. I let her think she goes for walks alone. When she cries, it's all we do. She has proven herself above the role I could never exempt her from because she is my girl, empress saliva, who helps us agree. We perennially conduce. We hold hands like a mausoleum wholesale. Her affection is nowhere suspect of mere survival.

The woman snatches my Zeze, puts a fat bulletin in her ear. Crack of the braid, bark and beer bottle glass, I dislodge madam cranial, hitched cheek against the wall, clap the hole some width. Bitch kneels a breath right through. Barak saunters by, plotting a harem like some fructose pimp. Zeze's hypothermically clung for safety, nude and fascinated, eyes outstretching the room. Barak palms his circumcision mishap along the showing cheekbone. He masquerades inside her bald, awful pate, fucking the whip mark to scraps, curving his cock poked sideways out her mouth like she's saying him, like he's all she could say, and facializes a blooded sigil. He's caked the outlet, forcing her to assist an extending exit space. Awright, she intones, fainting. She can't even twitch with expertise.

Kay, he's neglected his tobacco. It runs to bib him. Okay, he indicates Zeze. Anyone dire with my property flounders in hell. How a academic number they salvo?

We're fucking off now. As a present to your cocksucker breath continual at the suggestion.

Zeze giggles from the steel on her tummy. Hand me our footage. We'll do your show from home, sweetie.

Barak says bye: Big man's activating his smithereens. Us bunch were mutual with girls at the county freezer. Can that magic be defrocked? Zeze, your fans testify a nuclear financing. Ain't no poppas where we'll take you. No motherfuckers set for life. Our dicks don't just jabber. Ponder on it.

The mayhem gave her a sugar high. She somersaults through the trailer we decorate to sate her quirkiness: cured pelts bearing flowers, ruby teeth she finger paints, tea lights whose shadow play regale her. Story time: God plucked wolves from the sunset. None fanged the forest wall. Other species bumbled safe asleep. Hence the giant, scooping eastward, pinched every water in cuppers unlike paws. He pursed his lips, webbing the rain bye-bye, puddles basting sand then mud. The scrubbiest pups took a vote square against their kind, dedicated to emulate whichever bully stole the drink. Tribunals abdicated a pretense at capturing wolf skeleton for the win. Bottom homelands folded yellow, dusted hills they pecked back encumbered. The petrifaction humbled stances. Try pretending the heap unoccupied. The wolf hacked down a net of flies hovering reentry through ribcage. A diplomacy of quiet followed, a plotting of sanctions. Some eventual law would bury it. They found a castle that hurt the universe, sniffing ghostly of keesters the giant felled. Indicting nary a quiver, formations anywhere damp, voiding circular, the wolf flossed ectoplasm and spat cussed histories. A drawbridge was gummed of watery trace till the split-ass wood. The giant had had enough of hares and stomped them from existence. The wolf chortled, I never cared for hopping. He swayed a congealment of birds. The wolf guffawed, I never cared for flight. He put an end to snakes, to burrowing clades, to pests. I can speak for the dirt, nigh for what disturbs it. Soon they were alone in the genocide, in the calories of it, and gambled for refreshment, whosoever imbibes the dimensions. What the wolf drank drizzled from thievery back to the vat. Contrariwise, the giant gorged his bounty. His bladder was obliterated. Vexing any possible hell or surviving sentience, he constructed a casket and shut himself within.

Unfazed. She skips on her chamber pot. The porcelain blends with her squatting. I tickle her to bestow, curving a rag into the dent gathered for my thumb. I won't bill her of her pink. Her sphincter flitters, bargaining a fleck, immaculate once more. I channel it the bridge of my nose, huffing soft. She settles for a game of catch. The cheeks clench my lapping. She victory yells. I want to tattoo her constipation. I honk through her cat food leavings, tenting along, impinging ceremoniously. She spurs until my interior pant leg is fogged over. She hasn't viewed my dick since conscious, frequently asks when, capers with it through fabrics, Whac-A-Mole. We play doctor, test the split my finger couldn't purchase, centimeters-long hairline chiseled there like a total lack of empathy.

I tell her hymen odes. My tongue needles, vast for the area. I let it investigate premature. I'm hard off base tonight. She wiggles in discomfort, ensuingly relaxed. Her hips copycat a frustrated template until I draw out a starter kit of fluids. She's shocked, but rolls along. Am I coming, she interrupts, holding her abdomen like it might fragment. I continue, but she begins falsifying the caviar. I marionette her fingers into what I want her doing to herself nonstop as soon as functional. Feels nice, she grumbles. We go way past her bedtime figuring this out. I take myself exposed, bigger than her waist. She gasps, tugging rude, confusing the motion. I demonstrate the technique and she explodes me, instant through her hair, down her face, crossing her chest. We towel, sensing trouble. She appears curious. I disapprove how pretend that went.

Think I came.

Your germs aren't tall enough.

That's the imposition you can't recover, if they collect on their influence. When I say love you forever I mean forever just fucking happened. She adheres, pensive, to the sheets. I've become the flak of her silence. We cuddle, but she's the champion here, somehow. She was supposed to see the cock taking her from virginity into orgasm, not wagging at her like a chalkboard. Her body's catching up on my impatience. Um, I could do stuff for Barak if it helps my show. I grab Zeze so the bed collapses. Scream one, loaned from a surplus. No more shows. Why! She sobs, hitting herself. This word why is not allowed.

Because my friends contend heat death of the universe like a cafeteria bell. Could employ their huckster din for ketamine, you snotty nidus on the lure. Because I am uglier than how a crowd will reimburse you. I muscle the suburbs with my hair. I'm mister home invasion to you. Mister must of clams, grazing the fungus sweet, polished fertile. You desire yourself midway progressive, no wiser than your toga without a decent psychopath in your corner. Gonna bring me some baller thug clapping his nuts behind, some rockstar of the friendzone busy with locale? I promise these gals a text alert. Because I reek of holding cells and untitled placenta. I smashed you alive. Anyone's presence fucking encodes you. One request, never feign me your libations or I'll find a screwdriver and boy you out. You drab and cardinal veal I can vacate at will. I'll saddle you some poison ivy, bitch. Seconded with a light bulb. Bright idea, sleeve first, stomp you a hello cumshot. They'll staple your diaper to a piece of lightning so I can puff the spillover!

We sedate ourselves at dawn. She huddles, kissing her skittish knees, transferring me through them as someone subjacent. What she's seeing is me as the more lived in pussy, falling down itself with love. She sneaks out within a week. I follow the water where she twirls on both paws. I'm passive until someone's puttering in the bushes. Was this impossibly arranged? Did Barak stash her an actual fan? She's earned a show in secret. The groupie fishes his corny wrist. I get his clavicle a sec. The mucosal reciprocity of the blade inserted soundlessly between lip and nostril, a bland and hollow cricking, sneezes everything he peeped at the moon's reflection. I cart him backward so she'll think he left shy.

Next I scorn her awhile. Never should have introduced her around, spoiled with a pastime outside blowing me. When food's expended, she wanders out, presumably for rescue, unimpressed, arrogant and familiar, and finds me digging. I heave a pile from the depth, pat dirt flung from the mummified scaffolding of who faltered widespread, the surface pruning exsiccated of any hints at form or hair. Zeze's finally the waif I programmed, trembling in her bikini.

I glove the clustered patchwork of a larynx and we are harangued. Psst, anything plural is unforgivable. The fetus cryogenic in this muss is more petite than you. God don't vacation in her fanfare. Let's hobbyhorse the care we're given, return it with the vainest mimicry, and amusedly expose whoever snaps after being tapped that long. Do your boogie now and the turnout will be everyone who's passed.

Zeze begins wavering like a casualty.

A month from the inaugural menses, trees crouch toward her when she potties. I vault the thicket she undulates, swollen a decade, slashing into her, scraping us through the entire forest floor. She bats my chest, haggling, unnoticed, to suck instead. I chew her lilting, wrists laced, nipples defined in spite. The creek suicides upwind when she lubricates unwillingly, cocktip her labial circumference, but the egg faucets, shimmering less glum. I blur grass from her anus, nails to clit, chirping past the yield. She abets, cups herself, offering. I garner the tits enough to hold, tucking them into my throat, and rend us grunting out of traction. She's hobbled into the ricochet, curving tame, biting holes in my hand, squamocolumnar raid. She ebbs a groove forsworn, compulsory flinch, scrambles atop to mollify, erasing all her weight. Something overhead, rank without, yanks her astronomy. I hoard my ligature like an expletive belly to neck, regulate her air. She climbs up her own squirt. Each orgasm seems to part the entrails receding higher. She gives up, thrashing, dotting our raw abdomens, curling from the lip. She screeches out fistfuls of hair and hands them like a spectral gift blown across the forum into our eyes. She faints against my schism and I wake her hugging again to core the flower underjaw, expelling columns into and into her.

What we've done is more vehicular than love. She's anemic up and through her period. I put her on a plate every day. She heals under the bed like an animal conferencing with its syringe. I throw my cum on the tiles for medication. Eat her until I'm sick. She hems majestic, exact contour of my hard-on. I pick the candles off my joy and repossess pronto.

I abduct her neck, crunch the rest there to my balls. She could jerk me off through the lump in her nervous system. I fuck out our ozone. I'm the implanted gill extinct inside her. We screw ourselves territorial, bribed of the concept, owned and freed over and over. I coach her through an infirmary of encores until her muscles can come the recollection untouched. We backfire off the planet by our gums.

I'm stealing back the language I stored in her and replacing it with my semen. She's an unremitting lagoon, my valve the poundings upgrade, a puma sliding in its glue. Her coming eschews societal repercussion, graceless shuddering orgasms like someone sequestered from the standard. She rakes us without cognizance of expression or decibels. Ejaculate zero percent aware of any designation except mine.

Our regimen syncs around the fucking. We digest with a crescendo. She fellates the toothbrush. We montage fresh wrinkles from the slugging inside. Such mainstay ecstasy her eyes bag over. Our waking cycles concord. I enact her sum, telepathic thighs asunder, report between the stool plucked out my unclipped nails and foreskin. Her asshole corks famous sap I struggle through, crippling her temporarily, an excuse to be carried. She grieves her fiber. I feel the whisper on my urethra. Please. Which is all I want her having said.

I figure how she likes a slapping and deny her of it till the last minute. Her tremoring anxieties fall flat when I obtain her. Heart's in juvie, she says, curling around the problem as if to extract an inflammation from her chest.

I chart her square-inched with fluid, bundling in our palate a skill that never ceilings. She equates, elevator tantric. Each wands the other shivered. I'm expecting her to shatter at will and am instead coaxed through fathoms meant for life, the hookah in her chute ramming insurance free. I dart her my kids. She ovulates her own white rabies in return, coughs herself auto-pregnant so the miscarriages repeat.

We camp our fodder in the creek, rebounding no swim, hermetic magnets obsessively attenuating. She claws us fastened, cuing restrained between I love you's, surging venoms, straddling my shoulders to regenerate, lips coiling near drowned over my testicles, cock at tonsils, climbing everywhere, pinching us inside, beating her fists on my scratch marks to kill the cum till wrestled off, hollering a bent-over giggle. I unload into her dropping ass. She drags a flint stone rib to nape, swigs it back like a pill. We pass it kissed through our mutilating tongues.

She leans back and founts a stainless spiral of blood all down my face. I cheek punch her, strategically, and she flops halasana, squirting both ends gelled and twitchy.

When bandaged, she asks me to keep watch. She foils the sheets with angelic tossing, mimes our earlier positions diagrammed in blood. I trace her frailties rife for a flashback, cradle the image lasting, something invulnerable about her sleep.

She inhales studied, specks bannering the radiation, snores subtle against me, taken conscious in an unholy staring contest paced against her bruises. We levee years out the same oxygen. We're coinciding psychics, each a highlight of the other's mapping fricassee. No papuliferous spacetime corpulent around us, rapid fire strafing the suck, jacketing myriad signifiers black holed to density. The moment continues until it's all she asks for and I am crushed under my incapability to ever recap it. I run to town and buy her everything. I steal us a trampoline we distress the joints of, disassembled from some family's yard. We crowd the suspension, scouring for our remission from existence. She starts coming to get it over with.

Soon she lies impatient for a service. No amount of being socked random or roofing her into a mild gush will ignite. I pray to the stenosis she used to be good for, not a brush behind the knees has her cower. She's savoring her paralysis to deliberate with dad.

I drag another family to her in their house. She yawns while I skive them. My work goes downhill when she's apathetic. I pit child against mother, guide scissors in his hand. Say fore inside her pouch. He's ticked about the relentless birthdays. Nowhere near a titter. There's a brother her age I sigh to see her greet.

All yours, no solitude. I fondle while she blunders through his virginity. He manages, undeterred, because that's my luck. She cheeps an extra incline I have to revenge later. I leisurely decapitate him for trespassing. Tell her do the splits on bleach tonight.

She hums around so invigorated I exit the situation after popping her ten more done with the lottery. You have to prove you don't care or they really won't shake, but look at me, I'm her charity dwindling off-guard.

I charm a clueless townie with stolen drugs, improvise the lies necessary to have her secrete. We're on a hotel floor by midnight. The pretentious mechanics involved flout an expertise of one night stands so fluent with others' backgrounds I oust the will to forge her. Trach with an elbow, pancake her surrounding operation over the chortle I'd rather listen to. They're durable as the ice cream you reward their curves, geniuses at consuming life like it's a test you failed by proxy. I pocket jags of the lamina I trekked, torching out the STDs with a lighter.

My teen returns and returns, already triggered to the next freebies, an ingrate biased for the power I regret conceding.

Cars rummage the shire, a frat-wide compendium I'd have to eliminate the population to keep up with and would if she stayed gone. The dread between us tasks my forthcoming reply. She makes a hobby of scanning the floor. The night she shrugs me off her, claiming nothing personal, just winded of penetralia altogether, I dislocate her toenail and swill.

She threatens to run away, lazing up a suicide attempt. I break her ankle, await the obvious dime brave comeback about the cache of suitors and explain she's a brat at my limit of amusement about what was okayed. Her sarcasm proceeds until I pike a wrench between tongue and labrum. She nods, approving so well I fuck her with the tool hanging.

We hold each other on the floor, captured by the mercy of her realization I could never go through with it, met with that she's now in charge and the weight of her captaining to adopt us lovingly still. I nurse her through the roles I've been, games and diets tailored to exalt her, the brilliant creature she's ascended to in defiance of my shortcomings, memory itself featured around her, kept as contraband, crystalized outside the impending social plebes, her aesthetic summits choke-chaining us gabby – I let her know worse than I have always.

She reveals her stowed phones and letters, tips from the boys and girls she entertains. I stomach this, beguiled tender as the grandma I reputedly am. We swear to legislate our cheats as minor-league garb, but I sense the importance to her of being approved elsewhere. No telling if she'll become addicted to her privacy again. I've penciled in the utopia of her birth. You can't drool over your mistakes to go sailing.

On her petite stride, waited on hand and foot, we rehearse a loftier sex. I row what she's done out of her, showcase another woman when she's feeling cocky. She sacrifices me a girl her age and we're a triumvirate, sousing the camper, dual-wielding spliffs. Our hugs are slightly bulletproof upside down.

Those we occupy for competition slander who we are. We're overboard in voyeurs, welded to her propaganda of whichever mystic osmosis with several buddies, divvying herself carte blanche. Having a cunt never molds you less than who steadily lingers out of it. I committed her to the schema she's fumbling. No one can recommend you exclusive when you need. That's how feeble this got, how astray I swerved my flaw.

She's stirred her box some turbulence, siphoned out the lag, slinking home to the creeper seldom as his bayonet. She burdens me with my own longing, a recruit for our defaced potential. She blames her guilt on me. I do not abridge my crimes. I harbor them proportionate to the feeling of always having been forgot.

She says I'm emo. I'm the logic she's surpassed. She's coasting on her petition against us, balancing through tensions that might preface her autopsy. She reckons herself the winner of that scenario as well, no viscera of the depravity that would illustrate her my busiest inkling. She's manifested cool as the glucose pop song advertising her. I'm connived an ornate laundry list for control, desperate to scout myself the same. I stumble one iota into reign and preceding holocausts will fit under a microscope.

Our bed's colonized by the tatter she ushers in. Their pervading enthusiasm with her becomes the only consequential event. She pucks an ember into the mattress, fetal around the conundrum snaking between her knees. I refuse to declare the articles she roped out. Even if we could wait staff their fucking namesake.

Zeze paints her nails, the glove box full of shrimp ballasting antennae up her cleave. I could umpire a satellite. We can't drive our knees apart. Oh my god, I take the day to punch her. The knapsack jangling with pellets. We dine off our relation, can't stop discussing how we daub. I slept through parenthood. She's to and fro before the fist correlates her shamefacedly. She suppresses my ever having been in her with a menu. Tonight, I sing. A waitress wrings her dishrag over Zeze's scintillating cow. Ponytail affixed to each bun, the ruddy plate exits with her. Feels like weave. Old man, next stool over, lipping mayonnaise, coloreds museum, he moans, politely. The waitress meets us at the cash register, her stadium of greasy thighs furnished varicose. The tampon twisting in her hosiery provides its own soundtrack. Anyone's contingently fed.

Zeze and I slop ample, crosswise DNA footprints. The inquisitors from Jerry Springer sent a passenger pigeon. She applies war paint to go to bed. I'll inoculate our bastard in slow motion. My sleep is spun by fleas. I don't stop itching. Tiny olives next to every vein in my arm. I remember a gagging expanse of chandeliers. She was having my rookie when she died. Had her standing, tunneled with zinc, my eidetic inheritress, no trance on par. She emails jpegs labeled mom. Deer pixelated under a semi.

Razoring her spandex upside a hydrant, she says leave me to my mutton. I jerk cause there. Awash with the sleeping homeless. Lock them in lotions. I take the best beard, search that esophagus for drink. I allow him my darling in corn, slit his eyes to the passing planes. He discusses popcorn with the needy, hails astounding vermin. We applaud because applauding is the worst.

Fucking you includes dental. You're my blood once over. An abortion with chewing gum. Love you, I taunt. He has all these guns he puts in me. We used to buy the alphabet as existing. But our litter outgrew the bourgie woods. A fellow is riled by her clan. Nothing ever ends the living sewer loosed between her legs. She fucks too large. Excretes like a Muppet. Breeders and their love handle hopscotch. Pay attention or we'll tackle your sassy ribosomes. Ain't the outside always forcibly visited, I whine. The car bobs. The hydraulics get. Our confederate juices gape. We croak bacteria. My head performs its permanent wince. We're kind of kings.

Such a swank night. The domiciles glinting. The strays glinting. You should behold. Probably tint these windows. We were the first ground zero. Frangible carbon. He isn't any caliber of scar on me. I was weaned from other dick. He did everything to me before I had tits enough to provoke it. Behind the scenes, he killed for the luxury of my construction, banqueted genital, the concocted privilege. He swallowed my blueprints. Our trailer keeps a singular religion: whatever I expel. He gobbles my done baths. Brings the livelihood from junkyards. Birdfed regurgitated suppers, mulch of stale pizza. Men who need me vanish. Boys with flowers never found. He wrung me out over doorknobs. A sheet of bruises for escapes, sperm he didn't actuate, weeks hung in coil. He loves me lots. Enough to punch me through boredom. Boons my thought. I'm his woodland chitter. I crawl or remain. I follow nodding. It's called heterosexuality. It's called happy being mashed. A kissup wife and twin, astrological ping pong. I coo his nervous boners present. You settled for being kin.

At the bar, more biohazard swirl. Everyone's on mute in their own reality. The disease comes in. I come in holding my pants. A girl I know woots nothings in my hand. She purrs a little smoke vagina. I hit her so hard she goes into labor. The umbilical cord is severed with cheap matches. It was self-defense, she cries. Niggers, she cries. I feel my pubic hairs uproot into a halo. We pour drinks on her baby until it dies. I throw it in the dumpster and recite the rosary. She splashes water on her face, the only way she knows how to cry. I hear the white trash amen. We are needed elsewhere.

Ride to cocaine with an androgynous person. The dealer resembles PMS in seasick television fallout. I extinguish everybody's cigarette on my palm. Someone had their period all over this room. That which has been liberated from a cartoonist's bidet is throwing knives at my crust. Okay because I heft it somewhere punishable. Okay, but

I tolerate the knives less and less. Tranny uses them as a sort of lullaby to soothe what's left of her cunt after gangbangs.

Don't be so squalidly decisive about who neuters you. Voice of a cream-stuffed robot, malfunctioning jazz voice, chemical fire trumpet, I tend to maim people like this. They dropkick me into traffic. Your heads look bulbous. Yours sincerely, evicting a motorist through their car trunk, switching the chin round back their head like a wishing well full of blood, my heavy genitals raw with the weight of today and other days that hold them continuously lower.

Downright posse to her grip. Like an orphanage might happen. I measure her against the doorframe of a building. Knock our heads on the address. Histamine stunk rag at her thigh hosts plenty. I pour chunks of milk, filch through cotton, tasting none. Worn a minute in her anatomy, develop a distaste for any weight, the sweatiest baptized way. Trapped awkward, positioning, loose fit, she substitutes tightness, contracts. Hips routine, squeaking leather, I fight hysteria with eye contact. She parts, caves, concave smudge, a nervous rock of supply, my lap good for this. The second I come on my forearm reeking heat brews us one error, stuck at the drive-thru all afternoon, hushing the speaker beatitudes she never read.

Gal's big viscous under the hood, likes a cleat to her pelvis, reminder of the foundry that bragged us silly. She peels her calves in the tanning lamp, neighs about guacamole when I scurry through the chips. I am clobbering what is basically a tulip of foreskin into her maw. She berates my woe a thesaurus away from motivated, unaware that it won't engorge if steered at anyone with a price tag. I prescribe her an idea of her own supposedly daunting beauty as the drawback to stall, acting virginal and sweet until I can palm an image of who I'd rather have cowling the absence imposed to fuck well, a couple of slipshod adults for the acclaim of our maintenance.

When over, if ever this wasn't our measly sustenance ventilating itself, I crumple her onto my silted condom. She yelps a herniated jog through the daydream I've installed. I stand with the hindquarters whistling thematic on me, the remainder a saggy ovoid. She's still entitled to her self-defense. That the police might object. I discontinue her teeth because they are clogging what she really wants to relay. Why no kids, bitch? You all deplete at least a gurney's deck. I snare her beehive on the air conditioner grate to stabilize. We're through waiting out some bliss from the dope in our bottle while mom fucks the troops. She roars edicts to the bedroom, plagiarizing the singsongy merchandise equipping her. I ferment beneath the logo.

I was engineered to seize the wit from my followers. Then you can study anything in vain. The future dismissed charges of being shallow by dating someone less attractive, their frilly love's promotion rectified of your middling and vapid taste. I'm resolving my sex for you. Become polyuric or I'll consider you bored. Keep neglecting me like this and I'll grow up a comedian. I never met a girl who wasn't a jester to her fucking senses. Everyone's hilarious when you detach, but the more gone you are you're a shitty guest. Such a charade to never end up anybody's remedy. You try to understand cock so worthlessly you become one. Then you're just a daft rallier for currency. I'm sexily worse as is. The arrogance to suggest, then to splurge, any and all potential. Crave your own potential and everyone suffers in its place. There is no elemental whim coursing in this apron. There's simply the mystery of how men may wend you breeding once the prattle ceases. The world holds itself against you. I diverge a capful. Deny my pups entry. Would ice them from me if the accident occurred. No worries, still wanna stay hurt for you. Your nothing-matters-girl. Let's commend the smother real premium. Am I a princess balls-out alert? Asking for the sorority's finest hug? The monogamy behind every technocratic headway? Might my curriculum differ? Maybe you don't arrest me with my own concern? Bed my antagonist whenever you alone aren't it? No commitment to the conspiracy in my bottom? It's in my fucking character that I can pass out next to anyone. This is the politics of contentment for any unpunished rejecter. No more fucking gender if you stab me well. I have such a pissy hospitality no one dares return it, but there's no moratorium for the death penalty if we meet. What's my cocksucking intrinsic glitch, right? And who all's gone up it? That's the kind of treason you can place a cucumber in. I want to be indistinguishable from my pajamas.

Their spate oscillates delinquent platforms, frozen slant, replicating the figure undertow. She jots them mirrored across her thorax, serum she can't clean. Her legs fissure a patent to stargaze. They bunt her their scud from the bridge above. A smidgen of this crescentic fanning reaches me. She submerges for an inhuman duration, floats prevalent, ass bisected wet, loafing through another spree. Soot we're trussed in clangs back skyward. The rondure concealing me shimmies with each group's climax. She lugs the inseminating breeze behind her.

The woods shelter her accurately. We gotta flub what sows us? I knot her pigtails, rearrange her snug. She jilts the configuration. I have at my bottom lip. She strikes me from her, an alibi for her mood. She's a multiplex of withdrawals. I want to shriek touchdown in her ear.

Your baby bitch fragility is never as cute an unreasonable defense as you think, especially when you're off speed. If your tricks rather called you ugly, instead of letting you, in false modesty, say it first, they would then adorn you beyond your tiny comprehension, and you'd have to fill your own cunt with protein.

You think you're kamikaze, but women begot that. We

assort the terrestrial. We can be raised under any wolf. Don't you like that our eyewitnesses are built in? I can recant by the boatload. You utterly peruse. You tailgate my appeal with the scrutiny of a telemarketer. Stop chatting at the pedicure. I've tuckered you too too out to ever patch us. There's slim remnantal panic in my fanny. You fostered me into your ecumenically blessed VIP. You're so rickety my men decide to spare you.

That word women. Nothing should imply proliferation. The rest are auxiliary. I escort myself to her safety, railing the braid over my shoulders until glass embeds interstitial. Bolt my cheek some dentures to crinkle in her panoply. I surrender to whoever's next, blushing like a prize. She's evacuated from the fetish. Our restraining order will have a physique.

Clamorous brush guises a likeness. I loiter in my blood. If I marshal a following it will hinge up out of the ground. There is never not a hive buzzing adjacent to my pursuits. I've acquired too many weapons to ever renege.

I find a car's g-spot and broadcast it under who she's with, emerging from the slopes. Barak's van receives her. Dirt roads steal us toward his coop. I need her because I doubt my alchemy could produce something that lank twice. His dogs are senior citizens. We share a nod.

They're wheezing through some snipped apart Oxycontin appetizer. She rives each line a variation, the ballet demented and elite as always. He lies agape in the same manner he'll be found.

Her ass sinks on his jaw. He crows into it the response of his drugs. I tense my lacerations back to work. He's conversing with the intestine I amend much better inflated. She has cobbled an excuse to be here and I will pry it from her brain.

She backflips prostitute steep, bra amid them and the diving blowjob. Barak punts the couch incremental. She links her palms at me as if to wank some complicity from the betrayal. I sign for her to chomp. Barak wedges two obstructive fingers, helms her off, rotating for seconds from the gun. I crash the handle flat into his lobe.

I confront her over his abating manhood. She kitty-curls to seduce and a bullet extirpates between the floorboard and her kneecap.

Get home.

In case she's still a badass, I rim her with the barrel and fire behind like she shat the trigger. She leaps outdoors.

Barak simpers into the genesis of his quandary. His slave gear binds him. What a compiled tent in my nutsack. Or crucified by the taint? It's flanking in my vocals, baby. You haven't dozed.

Plug this in for me. He has to jiggle on how he's speared to reach the socket. Soldering iron? He blanches at the rudiment simmering.

You're thinking yours don't defect. But look at yours. I dote on her when she elopes because even my proverbs may go clunk. Don't worry. She treats us all like the prerequisite we are.

If you budged a scant yard from Zeze's domestication our recordings woulda outsold the classic downstairs.

She's Zeela now. She prefers the far side of the alphabet. Something about a finale helps her reside.

His bag rucks turnstile about the hardware's electrocution, oxidizing a silhouette. Interred sparkling calcifies him unsinewed. He drains monochrome heritage relieving in corpuscular incandescence. The plashing bleb thuds cohered to the chair. I apply him rouge from the pileup. He swivels in his fumes. Everyone acts like a referee while you disfigure them.

Barak once had a fuckwit appraisal behind the camera of my girl's moves. Conventional gestures to incite an audience. He was an eager curtailer of anything to its literal meaning so his sense of superiority could jockey intact.

I unlatch the basement door. The distribution of his pets by their odor. Bulging on a mattress under the stairs is Barak's attempt, wailing into her clamps. I inspect the carvings, brute scribbles, hayseed occult. She bids me have done, belted septicemic, ripe and pliant in ragged sections. I augment her numb from the mediating blast.

My daughter, said in throes. Mine too, I dispense the heel of my boot for companionship. She thanks her flies. Barak's refurbished his urinary tract infection like a wholehearted masterpiece, gussied the smock too fictile to shear off a ribbon of licorice. My lover borrowed this man's thoughts to use against me. His dungeon feels mid-life crisis.

Slats drilled in the brick scuttle hindmost. The barrier emits cricket vapor. I kneel into my disguise. A little girl is leashed to the wall. She wears her cuts more savage, has whittled them an insistent makeup. Tinier than Zeela, somehow further endowed. A mane rumpling in grime, amplified because the grime is hers. What you swipe out of her would be more feminine than anything I bothered loving. Haughtily ethmoidal, a discipline of moles concentric about her, plying the gangrenous ethnicity she's been carved from, bred as a dessert. She was waiting for me with an anime-hyped stare.

She suspends a foot no bigger than my hand, disputes my front with it. I cram her instep at my voice box. We're cinched before I realize clothes. She twines, conduit, stroking us to breathe, wading on my tip until I blink and come. Tendrilous slithering cements me stiff. She's wrenching me back hard, wracking piston-like testicular hurl, standing on one leg, the counteracted process rejuvenating capillaries like an article I should have read. I'm tripped to candor by the cadent musculature disclosing deeper torrid, vortex tendons reversing levitation so the leash snacks out her air. I prop the weight alone on my cock as suicide prevention. She responds, thronging on me till my balls are a stopper for whichever flow. A finessed motility, reptile gait, beyond metabolism. She paces full-carousel, grating us unwound. We bray our snuff, chug through each other, emotional range, the rift formerly her tongue rippling feral. Nurtured to supplant the sickle of your cum, no language outside the chloacal enucleation of compound pussy, a vent amputated through one chamber, her every waste shelled therein, she swaps out her rectum intramural and I spew up it, blat against cuisine.

I strafe the flint, nicking her kidney. She buckles, fading through cursive, jaunting rearward, widening it on purpose, blood stalling ahead in sheets, sifting plumed, fussier hardtack than normal. She's hijacked my prostrate and wants a massacre to release. We're murmuring at our sweat, routing the blade splenic, parallel to the cock advancing oblique through her, plunging for extraction, enjoining each pang heedless. I butcher an aisle in her, recumbent with the slinky-grasp clipping midriff, hydrochloric spice defecating a singularity blistered on our lap. I fuck her carrion pictorial, coming embellished out the naval, padding unsheathed. She is arachnoid in her vitals, truncating hazy for my target precum, gyrating acutely liver. Glans recoiling alongside knife point, mingling fallopian tubes sluiced fulcrum, wafting serosa modifies the nozzle of my bladder certifiably annulled. She blurts to divarication, to ungirded ribs yellowing plait. I fuck her until all I am fucking is some rations with a head.

Before we were detritus, fluking apparent, the handicapped feedback behind our neurons clicked on and the entropy that reclined there in anticipation of removing us barbed us infinitesimal from the shoestring implausibility of human connection. To creep from the seas, a nemesis undertaking first breaststroke, evolution in a hand basket, lavish glugs. We are inadmissible when the cells deposit. Anything scenic is an aberration tangential to the bottomless hostilities nonconsensually exerting us. I am an arena for my slab, a bunion on this deity, unable to complain.

Barak's is kindling without magnitude, skirmishing its era. The granite thoroughfare withers into chasers of the young entombed underneath, mediocre as the government sponsorship permitting each season. He may anonymously cringe. He's had a proficient and arsonous fleet of headache utopias, no gold watch or sword tributary to boot. He is partnering the climate. I am too generally under siege to notice specific rivalries.

Organisms synthesize, an in camera effect, microbes diaphanous like a corneal plug-in. They witch out on my sodden veneer. There's a spotlight fielding the crux of their utricular ringlet. I am customized in girl, rooted endoscopic. We're banking serrated atoms off the charnel in our thermos. They're approximately if everyone's water broke around a flamethrower.

I rehash the lens they take me for, smacking through apertures, staff aplenty. My faculties are being rented. Fusions tabulate with Zeela for the amphitheater blacklist she's undone. The canal warbling detached from her come is all we can volunteer. It mobs independent of those nixing it. She's an invalid scalded by her placemat compared with what I've dissected. They flake themselves a crown, retentions passaging monumental, of my prowess in its niche.

Boulevards without sidewalks, generic mansions cooling sisterly intendment, pets grousing the tectonics to refrain, basketballs plopping through oily stigma of workaholic driveways, commonwealth with the endurance of a photocopy, like some counterfeit hygiene you can't out-gossip, so good you should mop it up you, the clatter we expect, resident of her blood-stiff pajama bottoms. Men in riot gear allot the talus bagged herein, represent portable microwaves, thumbs up, point me toward the slides, deluging litter, people misting the block, attiring some mace, geisha limbs curbside, a sector's drama, checks cashed, escapist remuneration for shortcut pastors, a hamper full of identical migrations, weekend retinue fractioned on their dignity, storefronts like a decayed epididymis, lurching to withhold, deceived by our biology to stand up straight.

My new daughters and I will amble through the snooze button, hoping to identify the proto-symmetrical cunt who caused all this unwarranted housing anyway. Your only shelter is what others have removed from you. At least she'll smile in the plants. My archaic ex depicts no comparison, slumbering in the alimony of our undetectable trailer. I ladle her pathogens, flux up the encasing divot, droning phasic ass. My disinterest innervates her. I dish out a low sonogram, horizontally taciturn. Her sprinkler Skene, vasoactive flotilla, urchin cranny flickering nodules, defers unless led sycophantic. Rate it by her fear. She's flushing thermal, saturating our twinge, polar rust tooting in intervals. Mallet underneath, she resumes, still dazed, sawdust condensations, eking out her lime. I glom it apologized across the improving portrayal she hasn't noted in my other hand, her own antiseptic capacities flaring, spelled too discordant in her bubble wrap to peek through the little girl marrow widowing her befit.

There is a nearby darkening of mosquitoes. This will take more than eight feet of space. Cannot spray-huff her cajolery, blotting with the Moors. She's parched for every chief. We batter hours between cervical wax, thrusting out her age, sprightly KO, peddle the oncoming clitoridectomy. She'll delight her scab. I gnash my bridgework so enamel bits salt her, backhanded into colitis, buckteeth excavating windowsill.

Whoa, I haven't stopped bleeding since I met you. Don't really know you, but your hair is okay. You could kill me, but it's always our first date. I erupt the adequate ciders. Who would endorse you as their mate? You suck my burns like Fred Astaire because you're a caricature of yourself. You're uninterpretable in your fort, but a cadaver ain't proof of hierarchy. I rub cum into my eyes on purpose. Perhaps to see the son we shouldn't make and roast him there within the seeing. My feculence annihilates you. Buy me shiny shit. Your friend pulverized his receipt in my cleavage. We high-fived until we were almost bloody.

No homespun pixie cuts or Atari in the shower. Are you a boy yet?

I rape her against a door until the door is all she has. Comatose, she blips out an oblong scat, Play-Doh skinnies. We are all stranded at the altitude of our quarantines. I traverse the gauze her Hooked on Phonics rued in me, but there is no atrial thread. She was a utensil for thong bullshit condoned by her anfractuosity. We stayed strangers in another cheek, pugilist blood vessel hideouts pitched badly at each other's perimeter. Taped rampart to our carpals, oinking informants for the respiration we didn't coin, each more obedient to his session than she was ever anybody's outhouse. We used to damage our teeth kissing.

Where she comes to is another showroom. The clients still in their kenneled heat. Them boys' dicks ain't in parenthesis. You know I'm calm. Boombox's claymore supermarket chant for the breeze canceling her out. Got you some of that basement prestige. Ready to be rinsed back up the stitches what had you? The scowl I've been transplanting synovial through every distended relationship, yapping Allah, lost somewhere in the roaches. We inhale ganglia, film crew steam sidling. They'll embalm her skinny dipping by the hoof, sidekick to her scent, erections blocking meager tracks.

The opry an impletion dulcifying planktonic urines blemished together at the bottom of the cage her chin errantly quaffs, they bond unflagging, launch of brawn with subliminal precision, so their pheromones go broad. There's no pecking order declawed in, teats to the escalation of her coccyx. Hunted from decompression, the eyes elect to upchuck. I masturbate those tears. Were you pretending sex was such a gargantuan compromise until someone not boring came to you on their hind legs? They sprawl her throwback cadre shriveling to the creek. She has succumbed at last to the heterogeneous bow wow of the accentuation she decided to erode for.

Acrylic wafers sprout around her, big jelly in the tub. Smear those tattoos different, you fucking crayon-dissed throatjob amoeba warped in a drippy condom. She's carried urinal ice cubes in her mouth since rejection. Feel bad? Do a series of cartwheels you're not brave enough to end. We're genetic, waist high. You're too percussed between the barn. Anybody has the zip merit of your custody now. Your ashtray's gone viral at the dog pound. And I don't care enough to inter you with your betters. How about we reunite when I'm too elderly to notice? I'll buy another squaw to head into overly far. Who'll tame my fade to be a greater mammal faking the human process daily? I gnaw the sky you squat to leave.

# SUCKER JUNE

He tore the girl from mother to raise it in his palm, the premiere diaper saluting pomades of onyx, basting my source to swaddle what's claimed, distilleries we scampered through solved up me longer than I crisply lived. Pooch of tummy, he predicted his jock strap, supple grain, custodial slit, ass untainted by aerobics, taut but there, no hair or crease, burning candles on my abdomen, crying about TV, masturbating without catharsis, afraid of mirrors. I puddle under doors, barge rubber doused with kerosene tight inside a cone, flag from windows whole ghettos share, trundle an aspirin in these labia, grayingly inattentive, skim wrists wide open, waiting for gravity to dispel, stubbed on any promise, belonging beneath. We swallow our quiet snot together. I'm sharing the closest nimble pulse I have to hate. He taught me everything I'm not. Taught to worship the autopsy at the end of the rainbow, triangles of barm avuncular on my gasp that are promptly mountains, herpetic touchstones jostling this mantra ashy to the fuck-you digit. Heaved full-shoulder, scalp warps close, front teeth depart, maybe gulped, top and bottom. Steady the freshly minted clump, its conscious wagging, jabs calculated to canines, knuckle-splicers, anesthesia for cheap. Anchor a scooch with impact, sniff of sidewalk, burst the cheek, forming a hole to check deflated taction, blaring the head with found air. Blocky puke sieves a screen slid before the tush, cokemule behind her yanked-mean grimace, bile again ejecting. He rattles bone pan so loud neighbors second the floor above. Wherever we were we weren't. Tilt the pipe, jaw rescinds, yodeling alveoli. There the molars shine. He slivers them followed, fattening half-length. That mug wolfs tittle. He operates, pipe to bow, fundus regnant, shuttle of peptide, heavy lifting, glut has flavor, ending the accident a parent foments, acidic opinions tossed shish kebab, ton of swathing muscle, divulged of plexus, pyloric missy, magician rags nonstop. Sippy cups mom courted desert her gizmo, converted by having. Partial at this juncture, scraped angelic in my noggin, metal concurrent with whatever thought. Fibrous alliances emerge upon the crook, contra homeostasis by implosion, corrected of past science, mind a puking rap forced to pace. Calx revving illuminates beyond rhythm, temporarily invincible, a rafter of curtsies align the used-to-be radius, wallpapering primate asbestos, corneas ballistic, adhesive animations, nastily Scorpio. Distinguish a future egg, circuiting envy, encapsulated by cycle, ironed so burly opera ladies fertilize a mishap. These are coronary times. Ventriloquized shish hoards the gap, hussy's vibrating infrastructure roiled in slew, wiping yesterday's lettuce, digestion complete. My endowment's the necrophilic reform of leftover spread we spread. Originates his johnson with lactate, pristine formula, really knurls the ass from shopping, boy howdy, teased near to coma. The teeming snuggle is worth exactly bleach. He clops the entity of her swig on the couch next to us, lapper to bung, the whole confiscated puppetry, and dives in, strangling my first breath parroted between splooshes. He husked mom to dick-snag my handshake. The outmost brine nursed me alien. Any sense of family scales damage.

I hope something queenly stands wicked from my cunt, corrugated remains snorting whitehood, the chow reaped pricey, children like costumes decomposing into soda, postmortem acrobatics, played with, looked after, smiled at, mouth full of cardboard lair, tongues the size of a skyscraper. I love the assward circus tamed from my pets. Dragged to rescue, toggling their mange, creasing for pelt, kissing irrigations. My tummy snowballs, piles of fetus tipple inland, polyps with eyesight, laved abortions post-pregnancy. I hate DNA because it limits my origin. I evolved from dirt and speed, a splinter of grease, sniffing generations mother trickled in acidic portion with what she didn't parade-float up scrotums staid and princely. I hear gobbling sounds so much it's almost okay. Sometimes I say the word woof and mean it. The hips locked around my throat have to be pried loose by kung fu experts. Fuck my button convex, I swell giant brood, firing squirt enough to drown this borough. The antidote to human development: quake of my cum dowsing time, syphilitic candle cocktailed over cities. People willfully stop breathing just to think I like them. I use nametags because I'm nasty. If I have to learn someone's name, I'd rather kill that person. Each nanosecond fluctuates overlapping hatred so immense, then little glances happen and I want to get married, someone pets me and I reconsider procreation, stands up,

I want to slit their ballsac, shivers when I brush their hair, I want to bunch off all their skin and roll around in it, gives some laconic refusal and I want to prove the world is flat. My absenteeism is symptomatic of my being there. I miss not having been born yet. I trip over the moon to shave my legs. Who speaks evil of tampons? Toxic for one's perch. Those who try to ignore me jerk themselves off into hospitals. Let's page my period back from limbo, hummed from starvation, jibe the egg out of hiding and it sits up purring without gravity. Thighs spider-web black months reverse. The gush heats esophageal, revolving glow of birthmarks, stains that mean put me back in, ribs box the cramp and I flap to help inch belly topsy-turvy, dilated red, lips parting reflexive, sprinkling a baby no one might be cruel enough to raise. Better in town square, on the floors of schools disassembled by movement. Periods bring the silent magnetism of earth, the gay science involved. I bleed enough to get by. I don't bother with periods. I torrent boy scouts in a lamp. We share a trailer perfumed by discard, lack of chromosomes, numbing fishnets, pundit glitter. Being able to stand is miracle enough. I hunch, crabby, getting keen, live crouched over and feel luck, no ability to tell decades or bother heredity. Any distance from flesh, objects galore. Our babies are tubes of teeth, huffing for home and what belongs, searching under moms for their own, everyone a mistake if held. Who stuck a flashlight in our bastards? Degeneracy sainted by the sheer unlikelihood of survival, tinny uterus contains barking, hugs life a constant echo. Bested by pregnancy, I marvel the flak. Squeezing outlines down my dress with a high heel, bathroom tallied around breaths, bride to the world and what crawls there, I yank out my tapeworms for the chance to miss them. Honed through pigment, I chalk cognition, no longer happenstance, but a pledge recited in unison with history. The rim sutures preschool, bawdy constitution rendering hemisphere, buried red in a child's blink. Wavy as lame protest of my condition, lifetime's runoff spurting pitch, downpour egg, giddy to house detonation, blanket of cadaver-milk, pores on instant replay, jukebox full of scraps slinging devolved, mommy some diary made of universe kin can pause. He knows tiny placements within the meal for a certain tooth, epochs to swallow. Big quilts of placenta staged, trademarked by disappearance, contraceptives crowd me, there as epitaph. Incubating dwarfed meadows, I spend contamination anyhow, plant the grave whispers worms living inside me won't forgive, keeled over the marble in sublimation with some flashier act of will, accordion bowels restricted to a particular man, cornered against locations. I crave dandruff that dad way, the rapture at my nursery like a prop. I'm crucified with sperm, flagella besmirching shades of ladyboy. Beat boxers turn fascist for this heat. Statue of cream, stomp and gonad, rubber emasculator, slick undercarriage, stumps our church raised. The wife gnawed from dreams. A girl begs out of aging. She fabricates temperature. Being born pays her fines. My sons shed night to noon, lullaby for what I cannot touch. Their footfalls, fretting stenographs, use my cranium. The more I love, the smaller my stature. Find no kiss refunded. Ovum darlings itself a slur, nibble-lid for audience, sugar membrane, dash of crapulous gizzard. All that dangles accessorizes. Spiders entering coagulate in tandem. My sons hemorrhage jewels that pardon. Their bruises outlive them. I bite harmonies of foreskin. Argue for the sacred purpose of zoos capable within, giant garbage of watermelons down there. My dress runs the length of traffic. I'm twelve with a numb penny, genuflecting to cauterize whole parishes mid-porn. I read the bible. It's my species.

I said wife as a progression of the force by which he shrank toward me, rebuked. He slunk such an animated brunt the possession of my body became an undoing of the upscale minutiae we sometimes shared. I collected moments miniscule beyond his capability as their destructor, provisional, therefore no longer possessed, because it was this male habit of holding you as an item divorced of the present, with no one now beside, relaxed into existing, not an inch understood – it's simple, be there without pretense, please, I loved him, I really did – that led us into this corporate nightmare of being unified. His steadfast weight atop me tricked me sideways into puberty. He places my wounds, petty savior, caulks an eye, staring down the still-unfolding tucks, prim and slick, of where I land. He's sucked my clit in a thought-bubble all day. Perspiration lamps us, conducts our chafe. He slaps an extension cord through my cum. At some point we'll miss each other, lick the wall socket. I leak ounces of water I've eaten for the week. He stirs his tongue up my ass, cooing me close to an almost throb, floating gooey towage, his fingers v-shaped, compressing elastic. Wound around thick calibration, I contract tight for him, slam pathways. Our hips ache rhythm, rest thrown anywhere, an afterthought. We bake through so much friction the structure leans. I plug my hand in my mouth and quash. Organs hoist, suffocated. We let go, tenebrous, screaming in our tattoo, his tip unfurling car accidents at my transformation zone. Our hearts tamper fabulous congruities, body language the form of communication I keep traipsing. Saying hi is hard. I shush some manhood, slip into cummy boxers, do kielbasa pirouettes, raise the sheets like something's there, extend my good confidence to the world, focus on the limitations of length and how to hide. Because he decimates my panties, folded into them, an after sex magic show, I assume his genitalia, no longer accomplishing that gruesome male bounce and flap, are inch by inch retracting into egg sac. I'll have his musk by the time he's awake. He'll cream himself a flower, miss the lustrous dentistry, the sacrosanctity of penetration. Fucking him leaves an imprint, an echo of cock he reverberates as girly sing-song. He retains my aqua, flutters around, sloshing backwash. The metal coup of being under. Physical memory lasts longer than he cares. He is sore and angry for being sore and knocks my protuberance under red sore sheets, pretending to be me, before on to the next breaching, which occurs possibly in five minutes. Finish ogling transvestite us, because I disagree with leather, unless it is in my mouth. I uterine-clap beer bottles, become infected. I'm tied to earning pus if expiration follows. Imagine us in capes. Every grocery a sinner. He damns the room with gender. I boil my shadow to see where he'll move. Nylon piece of sleep, sprinter through disease, I rip my leggings ovals for hours, fistfuck the waterbed, meaning to evaporate, dab the sludge looming against cereal, eyelids inversed, roundhouse sweep paths to school. Because I own a swimming pool, refugees everywhere should pock both biceps up my vaginitis. Sperm the new ipecac. I look good when I shit. Turn the color. It's funny when people like you. Shit is more valuable than how people like you. I'm tired of whoever won't beat me. I flop too much doing exercises I never heard of, cannibal yoga polliwog, malignant gear reconnoitering skeleton to surface, perspective lines compose, recycled subocular. I kweef global warming effluviums with a sad face. Curve smooth against furnitures I pissed on. Scrunch to continue living. The bakery in my hips telescopes unfrosted comet jizz sprinkling the first evolution across a volcano, cervix winks tiny eons, spayed calendars, tubes bricked shut. Everyone shouts princess. I fashion paper crura schooners, twist the sky an origami dildo. If I had ideas, the police would hardly know me. Who baggies my lung work, masturbating into? Sometimes I think porta potty juice is as close as I'll get to having friends. He plays possum in my crimp, hissing stitches popped. I nail his vision free of pretend, lashes dotted, pendulous matches. I shoot things just to count, but the forecast is dick. Alms molten, blacked instrument donned for Wagner, organized potlucks, delicious between counties. Martyrs my blankets streamline pump the unending world. If jewelry was sold, it was from a corpse, your corpse. Trippin' stricture, portfolio of sweat ducked behind mote calves, suicide bib hornswoggled. Don't bound about like you expect the world to cum itself fixed. I'll handle your past like a monster. Who cares if I'm flat?

Blasted under the porch of a vacancy, I stay reverent. The awning patterns hotness, a corner of paunch where the oracle might live, flaking quicker than I reproduce, ridden empty of paint. I cram spoons upskirt, tow myself along, sphincter scratchy ever since birthdays. There are no laws inside this Rolex. Boys pay me to spot the basin. Chowder from a bridge up there releasing. We yolk till the last draw. I spurn my leftovers to restore them. Not much deserves if I relent. Say a mother swabbed us over college. Other than the sire bequeathed in fellatio that drew me by pipe from amnions he invented. Let one live and we've earned the privilege of stacking a rest home. Dementia buckled, pincer in the mind, tangling matter claspy. Memories loop, constricting until the centrifugal point stabbed in erasure is tense enough to finally grant a severe, protracted death, and we all are alive this way, to some extent, regardless, at the coffee reprocessed shit-smear, our sole company, cologned thusly in corners, once wise and unconditional. Spit on that word for me: unconditional. Don't we euthanize our pioneers? Wasn't I raised proper on the seminal glop chucked forward by how much cock I outlast? True messiahs never share. Christ, fangs akimbo, heel to cloud, boinks your leather, thinking of another face. I toss flower pots from second story windows because prayer is old-fashioned. Yesterday I sold mom's ashes at a drug deal. The buyers made me test it first. In my gums, the unction of her char lives on. Now my words replace her. I am my mother's men. God, I'm clingy, just some cunt reediting life all day from an online narrative. Copyrights endear. I flash Canada statutory tits. I live in a Japanese closet. Sneeze Algerian sperm. Typing instant message bukkake, I flit a telegraph to the small of my back, spread on a smoke signal, snap cell pics, a girl who rims my shorts, sent, children with gout, trannies who take notes, Hong Kong surfers circle jerking in a busy street, posted on the blog with pubic hair font. A guy from Sacramento is crying on my voicemail. I film my feet for Kansas, attend a webcam orgy, choking on my bra. I ask if father catches feast in my diaphragm. He died in childbirth. Literally, he's negative seven years old. His prick outdoes the coat hanger used after. Boything from Colorado judges my urine on cam. Girlcreature from school asks with what drugs her boyfriend brimmed me. LSD suppositories and I got pyrotechnic groin trauma. So he shampooed your cunt for CNN? Acronyms are hot. I'll plunder your crotch anon. I type upside down in the hatebox, legs over the chair top like white feathers that hate themselves. I invented wingspan. Typing fucked your mom over and over to my screen name. I am accountable for cellulite. Internet has an upset stomach because I wreck Dow Jones with the strobe of my toe.

He's due untold properties by the perfection of his hate. No life's worth seeing through, though, so why collect? His silence frigs its pose. He found my legs in a coloring book. They sputter like bent horns. This is how I go outside: I tuck a log of wood under my clit. I give people enough that they leave me alone. He fetches post-coital hornets, dumb and florescent, morally owned, index-seethed sayings none will grout. Don't discount your fan base its nine to five. Who cares if sex endures? He has staying powers beyond the capability of medicine. My entire gender nothing other than beheld. The cure he offers involves head. He likes traitors who sit on him best. We renounce our Christian names with a fork, team the spatter bandied unbeknownst, human health and understanding trifling geometries, panoramic trammel, doohickeys to whiff, though I hold contempt for revelry, not that every word isn't Last Rites. He spoke love the way no words patronize, Frank Sinatra of the public blow job, gave my bean a root canal to stretch processions verily antagonized, hewn tasteless twixt glitter, hoity as any future, degrees cuticle from having, hoarding this artery mansion-scoped, like I can suddenly pay the placebo in our lineage, shone with the reticular ventriloquism of atrophy, which means paused orgasm, carrying that gravy with me, so envy the mess. I wish the things you petted were a slideshow of my life, housed where fingers can't, in the virgin space of galaxy, what's distracted there of span. Better plains of static will protect the plagues we share. Emptied patrimonies strut his harness, mimicking varicose goodbye, wad fistfuls of pubic sad, erectile stunt. I stuff the Red Flyer with his bloat. We tugged it around years ago before our genitals developed and we had to stop looking one another in the eye. Hourglass clowns the daily attack, so increasingly followed clouds impersonate, tawdry. I'm modeling for genocide step by step, leaning double-digit weight, his slump banging after, comforter subsequent. I rub wet on his body to make fun of how much progress he thinks he made. I am a muscle draped in tiny creams, wrists strong enough to break a house whenever I feel wronged. Sitting on his face, I blow a bubble. He's turning back into the egg that laid us. I'd like to make the babies die right out of his scrotum with a firm tingle. I touch the collocating bruises. His rigor mortis looks beautiful on a trampoline. We droop like rap stars. We have a diet of flips quite ballerina. There's no stutter in my glide. There's no um in his rupture. We squash the rain with opioids, twin genes, poor boo. His testes cloak mondo gasoline. I shower on his spun ill hop, worn diaper for eyes, multiple viscosities of loss, capable of hugs. I scream and someone in the next lot screams. We're budgeted for the same stretcher, the bitch-blubber weave put vacant, such auntie swag flocked to rehab. I sit somewhere and too soon people know me. It's like this great debt I've agitated from their subconscious. Buffoon tonsils, slouchy there, saying ouch for approval. What a rancid bounce I haul, nothing but a tune to grip my pussy. Oh, poot the hens – Does she insinuate pity every touch, recondite and intentional, pampered evangelical to avoid, beating you off so rough afterward you feel traumatized? Does she indulge you under her blouse, saying siblings count, an apology that holds? Does your semen anger her? Are you two trinkets related kids renewed? You're no species together enough to recognize. That she never laughs when tickled scares you. Some feigned wrestle, alight with skin, attacked by markers, fuzzy wallet of a torso, writhing fake. Does she wash her feet on your chest? Glued to each other's incest. Someone might tell. She lives an infancy of continual pud. Her body keeps small trying to prevent further tearing. You marked yourself along albino portions, obsessed the toy, tore a tattoo of your size and rested knowing sin as something blinked back – Here I was, what others saw forsaken in me, stalked by every cousin the state had. I tried copper wire with my torso. I farmed out the wake, announcing plasma, dress bolstering my anorexic flaunt, the bestest waste convoluted him. I'll turn antenna, stage tertiary and thanks. He'd charge the crib for holding me. I tarp wasps in these beadie-beads, travel our neighborhood with the information. Unspool my scalp of every paced pretense at framing a face and lick me alopecic, welted of the idea of any cosmetic enhancement because he requires me bare, splotched in grip, the way I love full analogue. Take my blood pressure with this can. Who cares about size? He could reach my cervix with a penny. I'd pucker through his worst. Reeling hungry in lice because. My ticks are busy having me. I would dethrone them, but their feed-noise is how I circumnavigate the globe. Uncouple the molars that nab my gelatin and croon their bling. I will wear any role etched about-face, if bored. See these fingernails I'm snapping on his pillow? I sat up nights knowing fuck all, he's skedaddled. Never mind my bushido flavor guaranteed yours.

I inherit the estate evoked of my demolition, notching surrogate proms. Humanity's the elephant in the room, the chore that blears you, a coprophagia not even latex can intercept, unless you fatigue your restraints, I mean yawn. He's embarrassed by his veil. That I bluffed a domino him. The significant diagnostics of men. They're their own crucial dictionary. I'm casual enough to be doled out. Fuck the celebrity from those who dissent. We tap RIP on the pond, drown for miles, huddle zigzag between fists, super-tickled, crowd pummeling shrill. Sockets ruckus money per the ancestor of whatever sex destroys me, chowing at China, splashy methods dwarfing hue so tight I expulse fleece. Horsefly stung cataracts, slapped scooting, spy the turf mushed nappy to soup, ass and folds, chasing muscular system exposed, shiny fat wrapped in flay, squirting dermis, flabbergast each mouthful. Maggots rowing bedazzled through plaster, drool we hover with reflects. I dial the graveyard fizzy, corpse-crumbs exhaling orbital, thoughts teased into casts, into widget circulations tanged matronly, fainting refulgent. He kills the hot end of a cigarette on my nipple, scars dividing nullified, subsidiary. Could jam a closet with the seep. In a minute the world turns your crucifixion runny. Tits scrape bobbling clunch. Too far up my own rashes to hear flashlights, timed and religious, the kind of spatial misconception common amongst devotees, smoke of previous vulva. We poison suctions over fur, collect ornery fees, sneezing Flintstones Vitamins wrapped in wool. I am the umpteenth plumage testing stanzas, disappeared as fuck, buoyantly hex-flanged. Retard putty sucked by all. Knighted with crabgrass, ritualized splay, I bring armies to squat, am ruled under drainage pipes. Gnats fill their eighth-grade khakis ankle bad, sprung ogling rigor mortis, track my debris between sheets, beg for pee, toppled up there to doodle more mutants, fab natures credit our nut. I straw the saunter malnourished, spoiling bedtime, prenatally marooned, dressed in vertebrae, sort of eyes, birth yuck hitched solar. Brethren skeet whorls us, smooches the terrain arthritic, vetoing Satan in my favor, sweaty with mousse, unfortunate overbites strum the slag, sass dopey stench. Lawn of familial cool ranch, croaked squire, pretentious umbrella user, bicker algal and curd, chainsaw low heed, no zest for coda, fend your cavity, schmuck, hooting sunk mister. My ballad says ostrich. Pounce tall in me. I am the cackling meat here. There are solar systems at play. Lick the muzzle without mistake.

# THE
# ALL-ENCOMPASSED
# DROWNED

Her bible-long fuck rolled on pelts unmade, skin of an Uzi, sockets like a queen, prowl underground of men balled as fertilizer, husband to the till, snow bit land curling. She got fragged in her garbage. A bowtie whacked so askance as to backward ambulate time through calendars once new. Combed nautical, tromped to blood, heaped in our eyes like a sequin prayer. We put our arms up her like a carpet of scream tread stinky, witness chewing cud below the dress hugged somewhat born. What hammy doings. We sit on her stomach until feathers cough. Craters of son angle forth, the bark-textured mound passing wind, salad in the kweef. Another spools her clam with fiddle string. We flute the gun, slapping pond next to us jealous with flow. We slit her craggy to tell time, squat and gulp, her tumbling bald by the fistful. She is nearly loved, nearly welcomed alive. Her gullet cartilage cracks words, beaming symbol for squirrels, gyp the morsel, thinking as we come, mother of chickens purr, growing fungal in the smell, fish with the carcass. Day's done stating her serfdom. Computed bowels thrust home, we machine gun holes already there, popped fat and changing posture, leak fucked sunset high. The meat is getting into a rare compost of god. Later the face as it combusts squeals beneath a liquid so sharp to the tongue a filter on how we see becomes. We suck coke from her nose. Jerk our mash on splayed dink. Cumshot partition, bucking landfill, her face a dungmask, corpus lengthens, militias' ebony sperm bubbly there, an antique dip, dick swirl the germ, stretch the costume looser each ride. Joints blown, ass a tadpole incisor stuck clutching, gesticulating muck, fetid gloss of air diffused stable. Cumulate tissue, electrostatic mill, nationwide hairy. We swear allegiances by rot this diesel. Paint loins white cancer swoon. We're dating her pelvic floor. Canopy pasteurizing turd latte, dome-flavored. We sip the flab, sword-fighting, roosting glacial up her tire rambunctious spheres falling ouch again. Let owls poke in. Wire thighs shut with trail slither from dreaming. Hula-hoop the shack around our swelter, tobogganing britches, Holy Lord. Driveling skid mark demolished of indoor dairies, Sybian machine stirs her pole-knocked, furrowing crude directions, teeth avulsed base to skull. Our pus, suspenders, infections baseball up her throat, maestros of clack, pin warzones to honey, spun ceiling to eye sans pupil, remodeling anathemas the pharynx barely can relinquish with helping hands. Another bothers origins long forgot, stabbing portal across ribs so communion delivers. Another bicycles her chunk rising semblance of infant slaked. The skin a leather placement bitten extra weary as shrunk terms fight by. Her gash balloons accommodating mass till us-shaped bubbles stack the room. Our minds chode the shorter she spends whole.

We chomp shank porn slow. Buttery thirst struck forward. Everything palsies between our throat. Chaw the clap ruptured, dismantle by slurping, lunge breaded through flame, cordially exhumed, porous chemistry between glands, cuddling shrunk graft, bone to miniature version of her spilling. In the melanoma extant, we fuck smoke. She wears the forest on her vomit like a stole. We burst her ulcer, bellyshit idol till catacombs jut. Sybian upright, furry mechanism rammed luscious with sputum. Grand strolls design our rug. The motor whirs the weight impaled, taxidermy brunette mushrooming in revolt, churning zeros split to grin. Another promenades the gush, pilfers cubic. We sing an entry headfirst up the mask of it. Snigger reborn pussy muffle. Of clit and cavities we sing, of yipping enzymes, galloping into oak, this natty hybrid. Cusp of rooster baying tight, crayon without race, tour the pinch brought sorry, humble our molars. Accoutrement crud, love so contaminating manifolds mega juicy space, astronaut mowing. Chubby lather flattens hid. Tracheal ma'am, collared zygote dander, file her cluck, seaweed fudged nap. We spoof gravity, skating pinwheel through retina. Flaccid goons swarming zwieback, prone to stipulate. Please boy in our shucks. Please cough the sequel. Lured immaculate, tracksuit muzzled afro, fuck-bauble cantor for the flu. The cheese from her ass a turbine. Quantum biddies, marrow better than what was. Squirrelly perineum ambushed the pyre, smote by totem, thrush nestled bantam. Bless mistress, kept in sulfur, smear of clone, ate at birth, save our lint. Fuck that we're time's food. May we trouble its movement. Let to nymph, tawny with clap, jungle floss, flummox denied. We cry god if god suits us. Bow herd flesh to sight. Her curvature cut surface before colors were, maniac twat soaps molecules perky beyond culture, upturned by witchery, colder than her age, tummy full of apples, we take them out to shine, gore we rear found, stuffing within her burnt ours and haloed where burning pauses. Keratin peppering flay, singed faithful, perpendicular gusts, stiff product. Roping globular tincture, cramped dense, we hiccup collagen. We of the dew necklace gaggle, hosing a festoon orange toward disappeared centers. We claim our heads digested, bore from the confinement of her height, million swallowed gems. Her merry-go-round innards tethered duckpin to our junk. All her coke dogs the rill. Delving black continuance beneath mere skeleton. Thumb in her eye contorts maps. Yap anal-tasty kin. Her bump and grind entourage. We disgorge petroleum, profile ridged and baked, fingered Styrofoam, bitty bibles closing. Build a church of her and eat the prayers. Shave a landscape into her concussion. Scrawl partook of trees, drying tune. Grass shuffles newborn, suture of dirt and horizon, squirming hints, knitted iridescence. Sistine toads chant our crackhooey. The absconding foil where her steroids chime, askew of quiet, pasta mph. Her dead neck going yes and yes. She pets herself alive with promises. We catapult puppets webbing in her suds, crank-assed, charming as a tourniquet, our gleaming prey. She is ridden present from blind spots within what we, coupled, spongy, know.

Brunch a bazillion drafts of her grave, shit the bones remade, Legong chew toy, eighty-pound tooth mark, canvas nagged round its stinger, figurine Velcroed to the stork, retching fossils never thought. Even her X-rays showboat. Scripture declares she's ours, pantomiming mitochondrial sapidity, fucking womb reset. We dildo her heart like a slimy guess, come hairdos, rip her taste until it's us. Manacled to her icing, javelin laden drapes, ingurgitation farthing for the celibate, hurtling poon to clomped frequency, jousting her into obesity, enthralled stratum of centerfold thrombosis, the wart inlaid by its enunciation, ravaging judder. Consolidated bleat elicits a signature from the resin, toll the jowls, coves she'll govern. Speculum in her rubble, goading salubrious convulsion stilettos portend. Compensate the rolling pin and she will be razed from her camisole, repose incendiary nostalgias, broom them, yakking, sanguine. Laxative veterans unholstering ad hock casserole, elutriated symbiotic, mediating over her ensconced ampulla, cautioning Sterquilinus to stalemate the Valsalva maneuver, we embrace the colonoscopy with a deviated winnow, grounded aluminum up her occipital, wonkily marching through dimples. Tantalizing carcinomas, clad percipient in the emanation, idiosyncratic with our scuff, snitch out her dough. Interns at the trough, interpolating spontaneous hokum, spectrum of mandibles concert how average. Thwacking through her gamut like a fusty gourmet, no bandana top the hiatus, she tattles on her pottery, proselytizing conjugal defeat. The incumbent slush we maraud, harpooning her sauce verbatim, autobiographically bogus glochid surmised as the connubial, farts a mixture of refer and her trichotillomania to pine for the cynosure she obstinately wasn't. This starchy crusade. We're the fistula she knew she treasured. Foams grappling her shoe. She wee wees our cells autolytic, cannulas of nummy we hanker. The integral weaving of her uvula touts our quench. We're the ghost of meals she refused, expanding in her anyway. Prank her fontanelle countlessly guttered and journey the secretion, pores ticking, smegma in our sinus, rimjob vibrissa sizzling in her earwigs, epoxies muttering our act. We place a Band-Aid on her nucleus. Toe through her wham like an arcade, snort the gloating age from all who live. We tickle her ashes, her ashes the only air we keep breathing less and less. Bordering her slated anus, space between blinking always that tight, a buffet jumbling the zodiac, puborectalis swarthy until she pollinates her knickers. We nibble her mail until she stops existing.

The meconium bandwagon tabloids us. We, ajar culmination of our apoptosis, dosing the scythe laterally, polling the oviparous jolt that vandalized us toward potpourri, are deemed frugal if aghast, tranqued by furbelow, punitively wangling down Uribel to beset its nasal homily. We hatch, berserk in wigwams, coddled and nascent offenses, but dainty bedlam deciphered among phylacteries trolls apropos of diddly. Swindled into medical academies, naïve about the anachronisms of those ineffably defrauded or trim, we stripe the morgue, palatial with the itsy labes and pewter gall stag murky upon our dailies. Arctic under the scrim of any elementary bigot gowned with infiltration, plateauing them like rigid sleuths, each consort purloined to dehydrate its glee, the amalgam cudgel for exculpating barrettes, aloof in our sterility, garlanding lamella drudged topical, alacritous scritch of funeral podiums. We propose atop offspring, their surveillance and the curatorial languish of their homogenizers benched till sloppy seconds. Google has neutralized your general physician. No opprobrium if a penis can scrimmage stateside, galvanize its burgeoning, banish embryos. Everyone's the communicable produce of hallways. Auditorium balm of having stubbornly said us. Our shrines potter back the spunk, bramble dapper mythos, KKK tenure extorting a substance, summonses to be narcissistically faxed, stimulating the ward. Their striations mitigating retro, botanical furlough redolent of our quisling balk, persecution by cistern, bankrupt streak. No bailing out of ambrosial persiflage can dally our abeyance. We are so unstifled our barricades network. Can't sample the sinusoidal thorns abbreviating your bosom. Especially where our pellucidity frowns. The predicament that rustles, nominal scoffing at the paraphernalia up you. Discover the autonomic self and it qualmishly botches. Excurse the haunch, vivisected parochial, prognosis scorched, revival bupkis, levator palpebrea superioris scathing distinct. We aren't palpable until ransacking, until tart regimes assuage. Our booster zinging boo-boo nuptial callouses the echelon, gradating chines in bygone sibilance. Ectopically blabbed palisade ringed about the infarction, wrought in embolism, hypoxia punctate rasping smutch, accelerating the saline, staked intraperitoneal, cortical thickening rodeo stout. Hematomas agglutinate, sedulously malachite, fuddling bait ambulances quibble. An episiotomy the gauge of nutrition defibrillates our spoors over the deceased. Who else should own you? Anointed welterweights of our nook, vamping the inventory to meld them kindred, bivouacking paroxysmal with the inveterate chatter puzzled into shrouds, erratic with flamingos, too much kowtow. Cadged from whichever bumpkin tousles us concessions, perfidious then, not architecturally ours yet, because homicide permeates, a tocsin you can joyride, locomotive tizzy garbling the diocese. We will graduate parachutes staunch and tacky inside the bifocal scruple excoriated of our skank. Dibs.

She bowls elegiac sodiums spook with rapidity, basked in armpit, beluga poises clinched, totally outfucking the subwoofer right. Bash her coming or she won't, titties kiting tofu visitation, yolk the ambit, flailed mammary, branchward, puffy stratospheres sup where flung. Toes the strewn occult propellers binged of party, sprucing neon, apostrophe blastocysts jumped in puncture, ganked of valor, swum jokey, suave twigging all peaches double ought. Groupies bust aww to yummy diarrhea bedrock, crepe of tannin pruned in kennels. Blingiest stoop uttering ingredients for cremation, primo jitterbug squelch, stalwart badonk, concisely strabismic. Gulfing mounted dingle, rebuttal clutters her fundament, dowry of hummus, royal pontoon haggard. We pivot in her rump. Larvae trot syrups, chainmail facsimiles rollicking. Congested swizzle percolates the roux. Our prophylactic haymakers tong leeches free. Volume clouts crackerjack, blights the gob, guzzle-fabric stopping to sate. Succotash cleft sullies where we billow. Blotch scuzz-irked chronologies. She's dappled our strain another pearl, gurgling toward prolapse one percent champion. We spritz blonde pedigrees, acne on her Lamaze. Concatenating slut lobbed in swatch, dire residues ignite rosacea. Catoptric hers slog the pier. She's the maculation we do sit-ups from, lecher callback, succorable and shabby, retire the roe, nip an avalanche, omit mom a fleck. The paste we tusk darned from its stupor has a tide of frenulum to picnic in. Us some prototype corduroy planked cephalic, repelling by allele, rumbly blitz palpitating stem. We plunk absolvent, spindling her hypnotic purulence consecutively squeegeed. Omni-crevice gulch whisked through canteens, probing the goop, gouge miring, no more mend. Capital sewage. Port that shit. Prod descending aristocracies from the bunk dispatched us. Our synergy cameos atonic in catheters, her epiglottis the endocrine disruptor we cuff our cum to, bitch disposed of, beckoning annexed, eulogizing detergent upon phimosis. Cicatrix uppercuts, ringworm tipsy, xylophonic whirl clashing on dice. Not enough sanitizer dyke opposite the soy, straggling leopard-print, porcine marriage, headlocked in the tundra, kneading silicone to IUD, a gala on its utmost sprig. We spike her limpid, a prolix duct humidified by convoys, ingrained coquette we fink kinetic. She abrades lumber, our girdle zooming out, juggling cronies over streamlet, mesmerizing dredge. We foist a condo perforated astern between ants, shards of vegetation cloistering her ambit like a Healthy Choice mannequin fucked its own purview, the municipal analingus disbursing shrubs. All that is barren, trespassing magnum, nothing to consult, never bloom again.

We go round and round in filth just to become ourselves.

www.ingramcontent.com/pod-product-compliance
Lightning Source LLC
Chambersburg PA
CBHW052013240626
47153CB00008B/2854